Totally Bound Publishing books by Stacey Lynn Rhodes:

Winter's Thaw

SEASONED WOMEN
Volume One

Sex on Summer Sabbatical

Falling for the Other Brother

STACEY LYNN RHODES

Seasoned Women Volume One
ISBN # 978-1-78184-672-8
©Copyright Stacey Lynn Rhodes 2013
Cover Art by Posh Gosh ©Copyright 2013
Interior text design by Claire Siemaszkiewicz
Totally Bound Publishing

Published in 2013 by Totally Bound Publishing, Newland House, The Point, Weaver Road, Lincoln, LN6 3QN, United Kingdom.

SEX ON
SUMMER
SABBATICAL

Dedication

For all my fabulous forty-something female friends
and family.

Chapter One

"Ohhh."

Tori couldn't stifle a moan as the almost-pain of exerting muscles that seldom got used kicked in. It'd been a long time. Too long.

Panting slightly, she enjoyed the stretch as perspiration beaded across her glowing skin. She strained towards the pleasure she felt hovering just beyond reach.

Almost there. *Almost there…*

C'mon, endorphins.

Oh no. Side stitch.

And a cramp.

Shit.

Tori limped to an abrupt halt, pressing her hands to the sharp ache in her lower abdomen while scoping out a relatively clean spot on the kerb to collapse on. Using one hand to frantically massage her spasming calf, Tori had to use some of her very limited breath to laugh out loud at her dilemma as the humour of the situation struck her. So much for a brilliant start on her goals.

"I was going to offer you some help, but it sounds like you're doing okay now."

The deep voice must belong to the person wearing the running shoes in front of her, but for the life of her, Tori couldn't look up just then, concentrating on her inexpert massage while trying to breathe through the pain in her side.

"Oh, no. Not okay. But I had a feeling this would happen. It was going too well, know what I mean? First time I've run in years."

A warm, sympathetic chuckle. "Well, you were looking good, right up until you seized up."

"I'll bet that was pretty comical to watch. Ah, ah!" The cramp in her leg spiked painfully in spite of her efforts. Why the hell had she thought she could start exercising again? All at once she felt every year of her age. Oh to be a teen again, when she could run without any effort at all.

"Here, you have to flex it. No, don't point!" Strong hands forced her foot back towards her body as her rescuer knelt before her like Cinderella's prince. "Deep breaths, really deep. Fill your belly. That'll help your stitch."

"How'd you know I had a stitch in my side?" Tori panted, curled up in as close to a ball as she could get with one leg stuck out in front of her.

"I could tell by the way you suddenly grabbed your stomach like you'd been shot. Now don't pant, breathe deep." The steady voice was soothing, but demanded compliance.

Abandoning the short blows vaguely reminiscent of those she'd seen in movie birthing rooms, Tori obeyed, inhaling until she felt dizzy then letting the air whoosh out. Those hands had displaced hers on her calf, and she felt a moment of panic trying to remember whether she'd shaved her legs that morning. She winced at the thought of stubbly legs then realised that her side stitch was almost gone and the cramp was easing.

"Does that hurt?"

"No, feels good." *A little too good*. The man had great hands, and Tori was starting to get some ideas about other kind of exertion he could help her with.

"You winced."

Great hands *and* observant. Tori started to uncurl herself bit by bit, ready to coil back up at the first sign of pain.

"That's it, hon. Here, stretch your other leg out for me." He slid his hand along the back of her uninjured leg, encouraging her to ease it out straight, making her think again about the shaving bit. Yes, she realised with relief—she must be freshly shaved, else she wouldn't have worn shorts. She knew herself that well at least.

Once in a regular sitting position, she finally got a look at her Good Samaritan, and almost felt herself seize up again.

Guh.

Tori was in the presence of perfection. It was as if all the women in the world had got together and held a summit to design the most gorgeous man possible, then gave him great hands and sent him out to rescue damsels in distress.

Warm hazel eyes set off by irritatingly long lashes smiled encouragingly at her, so close that every blink looked as if it was in slow motion. Ruggedly handsome features, smooth skin, luscious lips—and that was just his face. His short dark hair had a hint of wave to it, settling perfectly in place even while exercising.

He had to be a model. Or he should be. Him on anything would equal sales through the roof.

His muscular arms were revealed by a sleeveless grey T-shirt, which was rather restrained of him—most of the similarly buffed young guys who had passed her running today went shirtless altogether. It was loose enough that Tori couldn't get an idea of his torso, but she just knew he'd be ripped. Wouldn't match the rest of him otherwise, and that would be a shame. His running shorts were also on the conservative side compared to what she'd seen, but the legs kneeling between hers were…

Between hers?

Oh mercy. She had a man between her legs. Did that count?

Nope, gotta be full-on sex to cross it off the list.

Her gaze snapped back up to his, and his helpfully concerned expression hadn't changed, precisely. But there was a hint of awareness there now that made Tori wish she was ten years younger. Or maybe fifteen.

Because if he was closer to thirty than twenty, she'd eat her running shoes.

He introduced himself, "I'm Adam."

I'm Eve, wanna bite my apple?

Tori cleared her throat, all too aware of his crouching form well within her most personal space. "Tori. Thanks for the help."

He smiled broadly. Perfect teeth too. "My pleasure. You know, it'll help if you walk for a bit. You need to keep moving to really work it out." He rocked back and stood in one fluid motion, then held his hands down to her.

Conscious of her sweaty palms, she swiped them down the front of her T-shirt before taking his hands.

His eyes dropped to watch their path over her abdomen. Or was he staring at her breasts?

Tori couldn't remember the last time she'd been so close to any man. That was just sad. And the proximity was wreaking havoc with her inner equilibrium. So much so that when she finally got to her feet, she kind of overbalanced and kept going, smacking head first right into the broad chest in front of her.

"Crap! I mean… Oh, just shoot me now," Tori muttered, trying to simultaneously balance herself, extricate her hands from his and control her libido. *Not* the kind of multi-tasking she was used to…and it showed.

After she finally succeeded in getting her hands free, he brought his up to steady her by the upper arms.

"Got it?"

That was just wrong on so many levels. But Tori knew what he meant. "I'm fine," she declared. Wow, even really sounded like she meant it.

"Okay, good. Ready to walk?"

He settled her hand in the crook of his arm, for all the world as if he was going to escort her to tea, or down the aisle, and she dug in her heels.

"Uh, just said I'm fine. Don't want to keep you from your run." She firmly separated from…him. Hadn't he told her his name already? Jeez, she just hated how she could never remember people's names. She swallowed her pride and asked quickly, "What's your name again?"

The smile that never seemed far from his lips deepened, and she added lickable dimples to his staggering plus column. Too bad he was so freaking young—the only negatory thus far—otherwise he'd be

perfect for item two on her Sabbatical Must-Do List—
'*Have smoking hot, no-strings-attached sex*'.

Not just any sex—the best sex of her life.

"Still Adam. And you're…"

"Running late." The lie popped out before she could rein it in. And duh, how could she have forgotten that? She was Eve to his Adam. *Eve, Adam. Adam. Adam.* God, she had a bad memory for stuff like that.

"Running late? I was going to say Tori. Is that a pun?"

Huh? Oh yeah – running…

Tori snickered, appreciating his humour. "No, but you're right. That is pretty funny. And actually I fibbed. I don't have anywhere I need to be." *He must think I'm a complete moron.* "I just don't want to waste any more of your time."

Adam turned and smoothly took her arm again, urging her into motion by his side. That one point of contact radiated happy tingles straight to every erogenous zone she possessed. She shivered.

"Why would you think you're wasting my time, Ms…?"

Caught off guard by the question, Tori automatically filled in the implied blank. "Warren. Tori Warren." Tori shot Alex an admiring glance. "That was pretty slick. Distract me with sex and cryptic questions and get the info you're looking for. Very double-oh-seven of you."

His eyebrows had shot upwards when she'd said 'sex'. A bit satisfied she'd managed to surprise him, she finally relented and walked willingly at his side.

"Sorry, but you must realise you're a disgustingly hot guy."

His hand dropped from her elbow. Mourning the loss of contact, Tori was still amused when Adam cleared his throat and a flush crept up his neck. *Oops.* The connection between her brain and her mouth had never had much of a time lag for editing purposes. Which was why she spent most of her time buried in the bowels of research facilities instead of interacting with real, live people.

"Sorry again. They don't let me out much."

"Is that why you were running? Did you pull off an escape?"

Laughter bubbled up and she went with it, feeling fantastic as she let it loose. By now her heart rate had come back down to normal, and they were almost at the intersection of the street by the java shop she loved.

The hell with running for today. "Do you want to grab a coffee or something?" she invited impulsively, trying not to care either way about his response.

"Sure." The low tone of his voice was still doing its nasty stirring thing way down inside, and she repressed an insane and reckless urge to suggest bypassing the coffee shop in favour of her condo.

Tori forcibly reminded herself of her list. The three major things that would make this forced sabbatical worthwhile. She'd vowed everything she did for the next three months would further one of the three goals she'd set for herself—get into the best shape of her life before it was too late, have a no-strings 'holiday' affair and the best sex of her life and do new things and have fun, treating this like a vacation at home.

Numbers. Hypotheses. Hard facts. Data. Goals. She always did well with those. Anything unplanned was hard for her to deal with. She had definitely not counted on meeting such a great guy, who seemed to have some sort of interest in her, when she'd decided to start exercising again today. But she couldn't just ignore her luck. Time to find out just how young was young. If he really was closer to thirty than twenty, she'd go for it. Early twenties, she'd pat him on his darling head and send him safely on his way.

"How old are you?"

He didn't even look surprised at the question as he continued to meet her gaze. Oh, to have that kind of self-confidence. "Twenty-five," he answered.

He just had to split the difference and make this difficult.

Figures. Oh well, nothing ventured, nothing gained.

* * * *

Adam watched Tori return from the counter with the drinks she had insisted upon paying for. She was already enchantingly kooky—he couldn't wait to see what happened when the extra shot and all the sugar kicked in.

A bit of pink tongue was caught firmly between her lips as she manoeuvred amongst the tables with a set look of concentration on her face. There was something sweet and stunningly sexy about her, and her outspoken quirkiness had him hooked.

Adam had been running on autopilot when he'd seen her cramp up and without hesitation had gone to her rescue. His background as a trainer and sports physiologist, and years of working with the public, had made it easy to peg her as a novice runner who had probably just plunged right into her workout without warming up, something he would have to help her avoid in the future.

He pondered that startling thought for a moment. Yes, he acknowledged, he wanted to see more of Tori.

A lot more.

Her question earlier about his age had Adam revising her own upwards a bit. Women in their twenties or even early thirties wouldn't be concerned with that sort of detail, at least not from the get-go. So he figured her to be at around her mid-thirties, although she hardly looked it. She had an innocent, slightly absent look about her he guessed would have many casual observers dismissing her as a young airhead. But Adam could sense the offbeat, random questions were most likely a sign of a very active mind at work.

She made it safely back to Adam and set the drinks down on the low table with a relieved smile. "Great table, thanks for snagging it."

The best part was that it was a loveseat all the way in the back of the café, which afforded them some privacy. She sat squarely in the middle of her cushion, and Adam let his leg loll over into neutral territory, prompting a raised eyebrow.

"So what do you do when you're not out running?" he asked lightly. He was surprised at the scowl his question caused. A cute little line deepened between her eyebrows. "What's wrong?"

Tori sighed. "Oh, nothing. My career is just a sore spot with me right now."

Adam grimaced inwardly. *Oops.* With the current economy, maybe making small talk about occupations wasn't the brightest idea. "Were you laid off?" he asked sympathetically.

A surprised look crossed her face—her mouth making an 'O'. "Oh. No, nothing like that. I've been pretty lucky." She picked up her mug and sipped from it. "I've been working for a pharmaceutical research company for the past, um…" She paused, glancing up at him, and cleared her throat. "Well, a long time. And one of the company perks for my division is that you get a paid sabbatical every five years. Mine have piled up." She shrugged casually, but her frustration was evident. "So I kind of had to take one."

Adam laughed at the disgruntled look. "They made you take a sabbatical against your will?" An image popped into his head of Secret Service-looking men in suits and dark glasses, their arms crossed, refusing her entry into her office. "So you're here on vacation?"

She looked a bit sheepish. "Well, no. I live near here."

Adam tried to puzzle out the reason for her hesitation. "So are you going anywhere exciting? How long is your sabbatical?"

"Three months. And no, I didn't plan anything." She shifted uncomfortably. "I'm just going to hang around here."

He leaned closer until he could almost see himself reflected in her amber eyes. "Why?" She had a face he could read like a book even on short acquaintance, and she was definitely hiding something.

"Why what?" she evaded.

"Why didn't you plan anything?"

Her lips compressed, and suddenly she burst out, "Because I didn't think they'd actually do it! Okay? They locked me out, revoked my codes. I can't even get into my own lab or office, much less access my work online. I still can't believe it." She hopped to her feet, and for a moment, Adam thought she was going to storm out, but she only walked over to the caddy and grabbed some napkins before coming back. Throwing all but one down on the table, she started methodically shredding one into long strips.

"Mental health break. Ha! Said I'd reached 'maximum capacity' when I accrued my fourth sabbatical, and I hadn't used vacation time in years and… Oh shit, well, I guess you just figured out how old I am." She threw him a disgusted look that Adam had a hard time keeping a straight face through. "They actually locked me out! For my 'own good', what a crock!" she fumed.

"Twenty years without a break is a long time, Tori," he ventured calmly, making sure no sign of his amusement was visible. "I'm sure they were just thinking about the long term."

Tori refused to meet his eyes, grabbing another napkin to torment.

Adam felt an upwelling of sympathy for Tori. He had the feeling she'd most likely just ignored every conversation or communication from her superiors on the topic, so it really had caught her by surprise. He could easily see her being that focused.

"Hey." He took the mass of mangled paper from her hands and replaced it with her mug. "It sounds like they didn't handle it very well, and I'm sorry about that."

She blinked at him, disbelief in every line of her face. "Really?"

"Really."

Tori searched his eyes. "You know, you're the first person to say that. Everyone else I know has told me that I'm crazy to be upset about a summer-long paid vacation."

She took a long drink and set the mug down decisively, turning back to him with a bounce. "So, are you doing anything tonight?"

"Um." Startled at the abrupt change of subject, Adam quickly searched his memory. "Nothing I can think of."

"Great. Would you like to have dinner at my place? Say seven o'clock?" She stroked a finger down his bare forearm, causing goosebumps to rise all along that side of his body.

Okay, now he was really confused. The switch to seductress was a bit startling after her demeanour thus far. But hey, he was flexible. "Dinner at seven sounds great."

Before the words finished leaving his mouth, she was on her feet again, heading to the counter. Tori returned with a pen and wrote on one of the remaining napkins.

"Here's my cell number and address. I'll see you tonight." She took a last gulp of coffee without sitting back down. "Sorry to drink and run. Well, run and drink and run." She chuckled and Adam grinned. "I've got a lot to do all of a sudden, so I'd better, uh, run." She winked and headed towards the door.

"Wait..." Adam stood and Tori spun back, arching an eyebrow at him, seemingly daring him to interrupt her plan. The sudden tension in her body language had him swallowing his suggestion they go out to dinner instead of causing her too much work. He settled on, "White or red wine?"

Tori visibly relaxed as she answered, "White. See you tonight."

Chapter Two

Adam took a deep breath before raising his hand to knock on the door. The newish condo was close enough to the beach that he knew it must've cost some serious money. If she was a pharmaceutical researcher, did that mean she was a doctor? Biochemist? He sighed. Pretty far out of his league. He waited in the warm evening air while he surveyed the neighbourhood.

Just as he was about the check the address again, he heard the locks being released from inside.

"Adam, hi." Tori opened the door all the way to invite him inside. She was dressed in a light summer dress in some material that draped and hugged every curve. Her feet were bare and her wavy auburn hair was down, hanging to her shoulders in a damp tangle. She smelt fresh and clean, and he couldn't resist stepping in to drop a kiss on her parted lips. Free of any makeup, they were soft and inviting, clinging to his, and the only thing that made him pull back was the sudden intrusion of a kitchen timer.

"Oh, shoot!" She took off inside in a flurry of movement, and Adam closed the door behind him after he let himself in. Following his nose to the kitchen, he caught Tori taking a huge, flat pan out of the oven.

"Need some help?"

"Nope, I've got it." She managed to lift it onto the stovetop then pulled out some foil to cover what looked like a rice dish. "It'll be just a little while longer while it finishes absorbing the broth."

"That's fine. And it smells great." And it did. Adam hadn't eaten more than a protein bar since the coffee that morning. He diplomatically ignored a rumble in his belly. "Is it okay if I put the wine in the freezer to quick-chill?"

She looked back over her shoulder at him apprehensively as he went ahead and opened the appliance. "Only if you can remember when it's time to come out. I wouldn't want it exploding or anything."

He closed the freezer and teased, "It won't be in there that long. Sounds like that has a ring of experience to it."

Tori bit her lip. "Well, I've done that a few times with beer and pop, but never wine." She shrugged and smiled. "But I've learned to set my alarm for stuff in the oven." She indicated their dinner with a proud flourish.

He took a few steps closer, enticed by the curious mix of innocent and vixen. He wondered just how experienced she was at dating. Her seductive invitation at the coffee shop seemed at odds with some of her other actions, and Adam was looking forward to figuring out which was the 'real' Tori.

He leaned in closer still. "So, Tori. What's on the menu?"

Tori barely remembered to breathe as Adam leant in, holding her hostage against the counter. They weren't even touching, but she felt surrounded by him.

"Paella," she finally managed.

He reached out, a smile teasing his lips. As his hand continued past her to the foil covering the paella pan, she heaved a sigh of relief then froze in realisation. "Oh, careful! It's hot!" She grabbed his hand as he stopped just short of touching the foil. "That's from experience, too. I always seem to get steam burns when I uncover something," she babbled, completely unnerved by his assertive masculine presence.

Oh, what had she been thinking, asking this virile young man over? At the time, Tori'd been so blown away by his unexpected empathy towards her work situation, she had foolishly jumped to the conclusion that he'd be perfect for checking off number two on her list. But Adam was so nice and so damn hot, he probably had any number of beautiful, young things lined up at this door.

Nice? She groaned. He was probably just being kind to the crazy old lady who'd practically had a seizure in front of him, got locked out by her own employer and had the temerity to ask him out…twice.

Adam turned his hand over so it was clasping hers, raising her hand to brush her knuckles with a light kiss, all the while holding her gaze with his own. Those beautiful eyes looked almost green in this light and held nothing demanding, only admiration. The simple, almost courtly, gesture went a long way towards soothing her anxiety.

"Glass of wine before it explodes?" he joked. He held onto her hand as the thought made her gasp reflexively and try to rush towards the freezer. She relaxed as he gave her one last squeeze before moving to retrieve the bottle. He refused to let her take it and also grabbed the glasses she had sitting out on the counter.

Something about the way Adam looked, preceding her into the living room with the bottle of wine clasped casually in his left hand, and two wine glasses hooked nonchalantly in his right, made Tori ache down low. He chose to sit on the sofa, glancing up at her with a knowing smile as she hovered, undecided about where to sit. Right next to him? Would that be too obvious? In the opposite chair would look ridiculous, like she was trying to avoid him, she decided finally, perching at his side, but making sure to leave a bit of room.

He poured them each a glass and she sipped at the light wine, making a mental note to try to find this one again. Adam had good taste in wine, but she wondered at his taste in women—to be there with her when he could have gone out with any number of young, fit women, and probably had.

The outside light begin to take on a soft hue, signalling the imminent end to another perfect summer day. Along with her self-deprecating thoughts of a minute ago, it made her melancholy. Summer slipping by. Toying with her wine glass, Tori sighed.

"What's wrong?" The husky voice was accompanied by a searing touch on the sensitive skin, bare skin, just inside her knee.

Adam looked so sweet and concerned and tempting as he asked, Tori finally just gave in to all that he seemed to promise, leaning in to stop just short of a kiss. She felt the warm caress of his exhale right before she took away the last remaining distance and melted into a meeting of lips that slid right into carnality. It was as though they had both been anticipating this since this morning, and took full advantage of the setting and scene to finally learn each other's taste.

Barely aware as the glass was plucked from her suddenly nerveless fingers, she immediately found use for her free hand and slid it through the soft waves of his hair, urging him on as he lowered her backwards onto the couch. He settled over her, bracing his weight somehow so that she was surrounded, yes, but not trapped.

Tori could scarcely breathe as her mind raced. This beautiful young man was actually into *her*? Obviously, he didn't know her very well yet. Perfect for her plan, but it was disconcerting to be suddenly confronted with the means to the dispassionately stated end of 'the best sex of her life'. It was one thing to outline it on paper, but the reality of it was so much more…

Then Adam claimed her lips again in a stroking, involved kiss and every thought that wasn't nailed down flew out of her head.

The tongue that reached to tangle and twine with hers tasted of mint and wine and man. Achingly aware of the long, muscular body hovering just over hers, she reached up to cradle his face, and as if that was the sign he'd been waiting for, he lowered his weight onto her. A torrid kiss descended on her open mouth, and she gave herself over to the myriad sensations, so long forgotten, coursing through her. She felt more engaged, more alive than she had in ages, and she relished every single rush of feeling and tingle.

It was lush and every bit as amazing as she had thought it would be when she'd first pictured this moment in the coffee shop. Glad now that she had taken the initiative, not wanting the end to come too quickly, she reluctantly disengaged from Adam and returned his quick smile.

"Dinner?"

"Sounds perfect." Adam easily rose then pulled her to her feet, lightly holding her upper arms for a moment as she got her balance. The warmth of his hands on her bare skin perversely sent a shiver through her.

"Cold?" he asked huskily, leaning in towards her ear.

Tori returned his knowing expression tit for tat. "Not hardly." *And it's getting warmer by the minute.*

She led the way into the kitchen, wondering whether he was watching her backside—momentarily self-conscious before she decided it wasn't worth worrying about. If she had her way, he'd be up close and personal with the bare version someday soon. Just to keep the mood, Tori put a little extra sway in her last couple of steps before turning at the stovetop.

Adam's gaze unapologetically rose from hip level, travelling slowly upwards—like a caress—until he locked eyes with her. He raised the bottle of wine he'd thoughtfully grabbed. "Okay to have a couple of glasses of this with dinner?"

"Sounds perfect," Tori deliberately echoed his earlier reply, before dropping the sexy pose and simply grinning like a fool. "Um, table's set, so if you want to grab the salad plates out of the fridge…?"

Tori carefully carried the paella pan to the table and set it down before removing the foil and gazing proudly at her creation. The asparagus spears she'd arranged on top looked like they'd steamed to perfection, and the bright variety of colours of vegetables and legumes in the rice were so pretty, she almost hated to mar it by dishing it out.

"It'll taste even better than it looks, I'm sure," Adam seemed to read her mind, and busied himself refilling their glasses while Tori dished out portions and gave the homemade salad dressing a swirl.

After they'd settled into eating and had taken a few bites, Adam asked, "So what made you decide to take up running again? And don't say 'to get in shape'," he cautioned prophetically, just when she would've said that very thing. "That's what everyone says, but it's too vague. What exactly are you trying to accomplish?"

Tori felt a surge of relief and ease — that could have been something she would have said. Maybe they had more in common than it seemed on the surface. She gave the question due consideration as she watched him watch her as she nibbled on a lemony asparagus spear.

"Well, I've noticed that some of my clothes, especially pants and skirts, are getting a little...um, tighter. I do a fair amount of sitting at the computer. And I used to be a runner when I was in my teens, but let it go when I got busy with work and school. I guess I miss how effortless everything seemed and figured running would help me get it back. I'm definitely not in good cardiovascular shape." That was pretty honest, but she stopped short of telling him how carrying groceries up the stairs winded her these days. That was just embarrassing.

Adam's gorgeous eyes were intently focused on her. "It's a good start, but you can't just run. You have to take a holistic approach to not only a variety of exercises, but also other lifestyle choices. A comprehensive plan would help." A flood of heat arrowed between her thighs as he picked up a spear and fed it to her, holding it as she bit her way down to his fingers. When he didn't let go, she dared to give the fingers a light lick before leaning back.

"Are you volunteering?"

Adam mirrored her posture then also sat upright, popping the last bit of the asparagus he'd fed her in his mouth. Picking up his wine glass, he tapped hers in a salute.

"I'd love to help you, Tori. In any way you need."

* * * *

Tori closed the door behind Adam and leaned against it with a heavy sigh. Could a man be any more freaking perfect? Effortless conversation, manners and a killer ass.

Lips. Really talented lips.

It was enough to give a girl a hot flash.

All that, and a gentleman too. Maybe a bit *too* gentlemanly. She frowned. Weren't they a bit old to stick to first base on the first date?

Her mind raced as she tried to make sense of the chaste end to the evening. Obviously, it would have been a bit much to expect they'd have down and dirty sex right away. Tori felt herself flush at the mental image of a sweaty, naked Adam tossing her around on the bed. But a bit more progress in the right direction would have been good.

Her fingers itched to hold a pencil, and without conscious thought, Tori found herself in her office, pulling a brand new project notebook from the drawer of her desk. She'd always done her best thinking in longhand, and kept a boxful of the old-fashioned composition notebooks and plain old Number Two pencils sharpened and handy at all times.

Summer Sabbatical Objective Two – Best Sex of My Life

Tori felt the tension within begin to loosen at the sight of the cover thus labelled. She opened the notebook with new purpose and began to write, thoughts flowing into words.

Objective – Reduce the uselessness of enforced sabbatical, doing so by ~~soliciting~~ finding attractive male partner, for primary purpose of having the most fulfilling sex of my life.
Timeline – TBD. All steps to be completed and satisfactory results yielded prior to my return to work, September third.

Nibbling on the eraser absent-mindedly, Tori nodded decisively. She turned the page, having mentally debated the relative merits of outline versus journal style for the entries. Adding today's date, she gave a brief, factual accounting of her meeting with Adam, all the details of his personal life she could remember and concluded with –

Subject is unexpectedly slow to initiate progressive physical contact. Non-physical stimulus had limited results. Subject continues as suitable candidate. Next goal – Secure access to subject's natural environment to further understand motivations and tactics most likely to achieve end result.

Tori closed the book and smiled to herself as she headed to get ready for bed with a spring in her step.

In other words, the next date needed to be on Adam's turf. Time to see what made him tick.

Chapter Three

Having a goal firmly in mind went a long way towards making Tori feel brave enough to bring a bag of workout clothes and accept Adam's invitation to meet him at Del Sol, the private fitness club he worked out of. All that courage fled the minute the door closed behind her and she was suddenly thrust into a world of über-fit, enhanced bodies. Instantly feeling every bit of her forty-cough-something years — plus a decade or so — she just about turned tail and ran.

"Hi there. Looks like your first time. I'm Amy." A tall, young brunette in a Del Sol collared shirt came up and offered her hand to shake. Only ingrained politeness and reflex saved Tori as she responded appropriately.

"Tori."

"Hi, Tori. Where can I get you started today?"

"I have an appointment with Adam."

If anything, her smile got even wider. "Ah yes. That's right — he mentioned you. Come with me, and let's get you changed."

Tori trailed along obediently, trying not to look at the plethora of human fitness on display around her. She'd never been to a gym before—were they all like this? It was like she'd walked into the pages of a fitness magazine. If this was what Adam got to look at every day, why on earth was he interested in her?

They followed the curve of the building, and Amy played tour guide along the way. "Guys are around the other side, women over here. You saw the café when you came in. There are also apparel and equipment shops off the lobby. Did you bring a swimsuit?"

Adam had told her to make sure to pack one, but it'd been years since she'd worn it, so she had no idea if it would even fit. "Have one, but…" She shrugged.

"That's great. Nothing like following up a workout with a soak or steam." They approached a counter.

"Hi, Jen, this is Tori Warren. She's one of Adam's."

"Hey, Amy. Hi, Tori. Nice to have you here. Let's get you set up in your locker. Since you're one of Adam's clients, you automatically get VIP status. One of the perks is the locker you're assigned will be registered only to you, so you can leave items in it until your next visit if you like—shoes, toiletries, that kind of thing. Whoever's here at the desk will keep the key while you work out. I just need you to fill this out and sign here to get you set up." She handed a tablet over to her with a form open on it.

Tori worked to fill in the blanks then did a cursory signature with her fingertip. She handed it back to Jen, who handed her a small key with a big plastic fob.

Amy walked her into the huge changing room and showed her around, then pointed out her locker. "So why don't you get dressed? You must be anxious to get started. I'll be waiting for you back where we got the key."

Tori opened the locker, admiring the set-up of shelves, hooks and even a mirror. "Wow." She quickly changed, hoping that her non-tech workout clothing wouldn't get her kicked out of the place.

Back outside the locker room, she exchanged her key for a towel and water bottle. Tori raised her eyebrows in question, and Jen smiled. "You get a bottle each visit — another one of the perks. Just be sure to use one of the recycling bins when you're done with it."

Amy expanded on her tour as she led Tori — surprisingly — to an office rather than the gym.

"I've texted Adam that you're ready for him, so he should be right in. Just have a seat."

Left alone for the moment, Tori looked around. "Jeez, it's like going to the doctor's office." The almost clinical environment brought to mind one of her favourite, private fantasies. Suddenly, the nebulous doctor she used to conjure in her head had Adam's face with a wicked smile.

Hmm. What have we here? I'm going to have to examine you very *closely, Tori…*

"Ready to do this?"

Tori jumped, startled, very glad that he couldn't read her mind, then smiled as Adam came in and closed the door behind him. Her fantasy popped back into her mind and her cheeks warmed. She cleared her throat.

Adam crossed the room towards her, looking fantastic in a form-fitting, club-logo'ed tank top and shorts. And as he pulled her in for a hug of greeting, all she could think about was how ridiculously happy she was to be with him…and how freaking hard it was going to be when the excuses to see him finally ran out and she had to go back to her normal life.

When on earth had she got so attached? A week ago she hadn't even known Adam was alive, and already she was mourning the loss of him at the end of her summer adventure.

Not part of the plan! she thought in a near panic.

"Relax." Adam backed away from her tense form with one last squeeze, guessing she was feeling out of her element. He cupped her soft jaw line in his hand. "It's just me. So" — he looked her up and down — "you look like you're ready to go. Hop up on the table." He patted the padded, sheet-covered massage table then busied himself with the computer, by the looks of it setting up her file.

She obligingly answered the routine questions, which seemed to put her more at ease until he got to the part about medications.

"None? How about vitamin supplements, aspirin or birth control?"

"Oh." She blushed and looked exasperated with herself. "I didn't really think of those things. Duh."

Adam smiled. Damn, she was cute when she got all fidgety. "Most people don't, which is why I try to clarify. So, any of the above?"

"Um, just vitamin C. Occasionally I take an ibuprofen, but not often. And…Depo-Provera." This last was said in almost a whisper.

He purposely didn't tease, letting her calm down again as he typed the information in. "Okay, let's take your vitals for a baseline." Adam pulled the blood pressure cuff away from the wall and tried to remain dispassionate as he ran through his normal routine with half his mind on his work and the other half enjoying the innocent touches and her breathless reactions to them.

Sternly warning himself to keep it under control in the workplace, he was nevertheless glad he'd worn a restraining jock as he knew what was to come. Just the thought of putting Tori through her paces, thoroughly assessing her body, was severely taxing his restraint...and he had barely started. For the first time, he doubted the wisdom of taking her on as a client.

Oh, come on, you can keep it professional here. She's just another body.

Yeah, right.

"Okay, lie back. We're going to do some range of motion so I can get an idea of where you're at."

Tori surprised him by lying back immediately, without a protest, giving herself over to his control. Swallowing at the vision she made reclined before him, he tried to get back on task, running through a typical range of motion series involving all her joints. All the while, he was hard pressed to keep his touches clinical rather than caressing. And the little minx had to know what she was doing to him, a knowing glint in her eye as she watched him manipulate her body.

Having her stand, he ran through an informal flexibility test, noticing she winced as she stretched her hamstrings.

"Are you sore from running?"

Tori grimaced slightly. "Is it obvious?"

Adam had to fight a laugh at her pout. "Just to me. It's what I do. We'll do some stretching both before and after your workout, and I'll keep it in mind when I choose what you're going to work on today. So what time of day do you feel at your best?"

Regarding him thoughtfully, she leant back against the table, the move thrusting her breasts forward under her T-shirt. She was either a huge tease, or she had no idea how alluring she looked. Adam's throat went dry.

"Hmm, that's a tough one. I do my best work later in the day and into the evening. But physically? I guess I feel at my peak about now, around mid-morning."

"Then that's when we'll try to meet for workouts. That actually works well for me. Most of my clients work during the day, so early morning and late afternoon to evening are my busy times." Equal parts relieved and disappointed when she straightened, Adam forged ahead to the fun part. After rummaging in the drawer, he came up with a tape measure.

Tori's eyes widened with alarm. "*Oh* no. No, no, no. You are *not* measuring my butt." She began scooting along the edge of the table as if seeking safety.

Laughing aloud, Adam advanced on her. "Come on. Don't you want to see how much you've improved by the end of the summer?"

She glared at him, arms crossed. "Are you telling me my ass needs improvement?"

Your ass is perfect. "Almost everyone has room for improvement, Tori. Isn't that why you're here?"

"Hmph, I suppose. But I have less 'room' than most." She slid her hands down over her short-clad backside as if taking measure of herself.

Deciding that come hell or high water he was going to trace the same path with his hands—and tongue— very soon, he reined in his lustful thoughts and coaxed, "It's not just your hips—I'm going to take measurements from top to, uh, bottom." His mouth quirked into a smile as he couldn't resist the play on words. "Believe it or not, some areas we'll want to see increase in size as you gain muscle. Now extend your arms straight out to the sides." He demonstrated briefly before pulling his computer towards him for easy access in inputting the stats.

Visibly coming to a decision—Tori seemed to be one of those souls whose face revealed every thought and emotion—she relaxed and took the pose he indicated. Making quick work of recording her upper body measurements, he knelt before her and prodded her to widen her stance. A slight hitch in her breathing was her only change in demeanour as he ran the tape around her inner thigh. Forcibly resisting the urge to linger at the silky skin there, he measured her calves then looked up with a smile. "Hips time."

By this point, she looked resigned. "Ugh. Fine. Just don't tell me."

He kept the momentum going with a trip to the scale for her weight, which she amusingly kept her eyes closed through, and her height—exactly one foot shorter than himself.

"Okay. Ready to run through some strength work? We'll do your upper body and core today since your legs are tight. Did you bring your suit?" At her nod, he added, "Then we'll hit the pool for some cardio." Her look of surprise was priceless, and he had a sudden thought. "You *can* swim, can't you?"

"Well, yes, but…"

"It's been a while," he finished knowingly, then encouraged, "It's just like riding a bike."

Tori made a show of looking perplexed. "I know it's been some time, but I'm pretty sure swimming is way different than biking." The twinkle in her eyes delighted him as she teased.

He laughed and placed his hand on the small of her back to guide her towards the door. He wasn't certain, but he had the feeling he was seeing a side of her she rarely showed to others. "I'm really glad you decided to come in."

"Me too. Even though I really wanted to improve my fitness, I wasn't really sure how to start," she confessed. "And obviously my plunge-right-in approach wasn't a winner."

"Well, if you hadn't done that, we might not have met."

She stopped in her tracks then nodded thoughtfully. "That's true."

"Let's get going." He opened the door and indicated for her to precede him. "I'm going to personally make sure that you meet all your goals."

He couldn't have predicted her reaction to his encouragement. Tori went bright red as her transparent facial expression reflected a succession of shock, embarrassment, guilt and — lust? *What on earth?* His curiosity piqued, he wondered at her extreme reaction to his seemingly straightforward promise.

Adam mentally reviewed what he'd said. He'd obviously been referring to her fitness goals, but her immediate response pointed elsewhere.

To something else just as physical? Adam guessed with his own shot of lust.

Exactly what sort of goals had she set for herself?

Then and there, Adam made it *his* goal to find out.

Chapter Four

"So how are you feeling so far?" Adam posed the question to Tori, who sat cross-legged on the other side of her coffee table, sharing the takeout Chinese he'd brought along.

"A little sore, but surprisingly good." And she did look surprised, as if she'd been expecting to need a trip to the hospital.

Adam grinned at her before using his chopsticks to steal a spicy shrimp from her plate.

"Hey!" After a cute pout, Tori retaliated by snatching his egg roll.

"Oh, come on!" He rose up on his knees and tried for a menacing expression. "That's my only egg roll. You have tons of shrimp."

"Come and get it," she taunted, then squealed as he knee-walked around the open side of the table, effectively trapping her between him and the couch.

"I'd think twice before issuing a challenge like that," Adam warned, his khaki shorts getting tighter by the second at the sight of Tori flushed with humour, interested eyes watching his approach. "Now I *have* to get it back. I'm competitive that way."

Tori brandished the egg roll teasingly then changed tactics and acquiesced, melting against Adam as he pulled her full against his chest. Almost groaning at the feel of the plush give of her breasts against him, he licked his lips, watching as her gaze zeroed in on his mouth. "Bite," he demanded, mock-seriously.

Her tongue sneaked out to swipe her own bottom lip, tempting him to skip the appetiser and head straight to dessert. He took a bite anyway, tugging with his teeth before biting through and chewing the crispy treat.

"I have fun with you."

Tori's wistful confidence sent a dart straight to Adam's heart. Glad to hear her affirmation, but a bit concerned about the reason behind her wonderment, he grew serious and set his forehead against hers.

"I have fun with you, too. Mind telling me why it sounds as though that comes as a shock?"

Tori shrugged uncomfortably, and Adam intuitively backed off, giving her some physical space in which to think. The silence dragged out, but just when he thought she was going to avoid the question, she responded.

"I haven't really had a lot of fun in my life. Especially not *with* anyone. That's one of the reasons I..." Tori's eyes widened dramatically as she cut off mid-sentence.

If Adam had thought she was uncomfortable before, now she looked about ready to bolt. But he wasn't letting her off the hook that easily, not when he sensed they were just getting to something important.

"One of the reasons you..." he prompted, waiting patiently.

Adam could almost hear her brain whirring through scenarios. Finally, she seemed to come to some conclusion and confessed, "I made it a goal of mine to treat this sabbatical like a vacation and have fun."

"Well, I'll just have to help you with that one, too," Adam offered with a knowing grin, and he leaned closer as he continued in a low voice, "I'm going to have a great summer helping you meet all your goals."

A strangled little sound was her response as she stilled, confirming Adam's suspicion that there was more to her goals than just fun and fitness. If he could only figure out what she was so embarrassed about.

On a hunch, and not above a little snooping, he straightened suddenly as if he'd just remembered something. Pulling his phone out of his pocket, he tapped aimlessly on it for a few moments. "Shoot. Hey, do you mind if I use your computer to check my email?"

"Sure." Her brow quirked quizzically, but she didn't ask for details, for which Adam was profoundly grateful, since he wasn't sure he could come up with a plausible reason for needing to do it right then. He hoped she wouldn't ask what was wrong with his smartphone. He didn't want to actually lie to her.

Tori led him into a bedroom she'd set up as an office—he noticed a laptop as well as a desktop. She powered up the desktop, entering several layers of passwords he didn't bother trying to catch, and opened the web browser. "Here you go."

"I'll be just a few minutes. Thanks a lot, I appreciate it."

"I'll clean up from dinner while you're doing that." Tori turned to walk out of the door, but not before Adam noticed her gaze being drawn to a stack of inboxes. He went ahead and accessed his email, waiting for the sound of dishes and water running in the kitchen before he dared to look at the organisers.

Without touching them, he could tell most were just bills and apparently some work-related paperwork. But the top level held three notebooks, the old-fashioned black and white kind with a space on the cover for a title. The top one was titled in neat print:

Summer Sabbatical Objective One – Best Shape of My Life

Bingo. With growing excitement, he bypassed that one – he was probably already privy to everything in there anyway – and carefully picked up the other two.

Summer Sabbatical Objective Two – Best Sex of My Life
Summer Sabbatical Objective Three – Most Fun of My Life

Oh. *Oh!* Adam grinned and just barely stifled a laugh as he read number two. No wonder Tori flipped out every time he mentioned helping her meet her goals.

Oh yes, I'll be helping you with that one, too. The trifecta. Perfect.

Sounds of dishes being done still rang from the kitchen, but Adam knew his time was getting short. He quickly opened number two, and began to read.

A few minutes later, he closed the book, not caring at that moment whether she caught him at it or not. He mechanically replaced the notebooks in their original spot and closed down his email. He was walking towards the door just as Tori came back in.

"Hi. Are you all finished? I put on some decaf."

Adam managed a smile. Or something like one anyway.

"Can I take a rain check? I need to get going."

Tori looked disappointed and a little concerned as she stepped closer. "Anything wrong? Did you get some bad news?"

"No, nothing like that. Something unexpected just came up." It had been unexpected all right. "I'll see you at the gym tomorrow. Okay?" Pressing a light kiss to her cheek, he made his escape.

As he descended the stairs from her apartment in the cool night air, he felt his shock attempting to morph into anger. He shut that emotion down, got into his car and headed home on autopilot, purposely not thinking about what he had seen until he was home.

It's like that old saying— Eavesdroppers never hear any good of themselves. Boy, did I get hit by the payback's-a-bitch fairy.

He exhaled heavily as he let himself in then tossed his keys onto the hall table with a clink and a thud. Deciding against a drink, he at last settled on his couch. Only then did he let the scene replay itself, how he'd needed to leave Tori's *right then*, in order to process what he'd read—a very cold-blooded plan for seduction.

Of which *he* was the object. Pun intended.

It had all been neatly laid out, how she had decided after meeting Adam that he would fit the bill, her wishing that things would progress faster—after all, sex *must* be had before September!—and the final extra little detail that had really thrown him.

This—their 'relationship'—was a means to an end. And when the sex finally happened, the *end* is exactly what it would be.

To a 'no-strings holiday affair'.

It was bizarre being on the other end of sex for sex's sake. Adam gave a humourless little laugh at the irony of it all. He'd been taking it slow because he thought he'd found in Tori a woman he could develop something long term with. And with her being older and more mature than his usual dates, he'd assumed she would be receptive to the slower pacing and a possible commitment.

In the meantime, she'd been sizing him up for a summer fling.

Adam rolled his eyes heavenward.

What the hell kind of twisted karma was that?

He briefly considered just going with the flow and giving her exactly what she wanted—what just about any other twenty-something guy would happily go along with—a no-strings affair, NSA to use personal ad-speak. That, to him, felt about as impersonal and tawdry as a personal ad would. As that pettiness occurred to him, Adam was already shaking his head, trying to banish the foul thought. *Yuck. No thanks.* He couldn't pull a wham, bam, thank you ma'am on his quirky, sweet Tori. Even if that's what she had in her head that she wanted.

It just didn't make sense to him. Why the hell would Tori be on the prowl for a one-off? She was such a sweetheart. Classy, funny, smart...

The wave of tenderness that hit him at the reminder of his original assessment of her had a clarifying effect. Something had been nagging him about his discovery ever since he'd read the journal, or whatever it was called. The seemingly heartless and clinical approach to the very personal objective.

He seized onto the word 'clinical'. Maybe that was just how she broke things down. She was a scientist. Perhaps she thought she could plan best when the emotional and subjective qualifiers were removed. Adam thought about his own background in science. He never would have thought about applying the scientific method to something so far removed—in his mind—from the sterility of an experiment.

But now that he'd thought of it, Adam would bet Tori would.

He had to get a look at the other two notebooks. If they also read as matter-of-factly as an English translation of foreign assembly instructions, then he would know for sure.

In the meantime, he needed to decide how to handle Tori's need to rush to the finish line.

Adam smiled a little as he rose to go find a sheet of paper and a pen to do a little planning of his own.

One thing he *wouldn't* do was have sex with her before the end of summer. No matter how hard she tried.

Chapter Five

Tori looked around her condo with a sigh. It was cleaned to within an inch of its life and everything was in its place. She'd rearranged the furniture a couple of times and now had it the way she liked it. But the walls were starting to close in and the day loomed before her.

I'm so freaking bored.

She was not used to having that kind of problem. When she was working her usual long hours, she barely had the energy to cook dinner and keep up with her bills and paperwork on weeknights. The weekends, when she didn't spend them working, were consumed with cleaning and shopping and the odd, very seldom social engagement.

Now, she had all the time in the world. And she was fast becoming reliant on Adam to fill the void. But he had to work with his other clients sometime, and today was one of those days—what he called a 'rest day' for her workout regime, which meant she had no real reason to see him at all today. It was also the day of the week where he had his latest appointments, so they hadn't made any firm plans for the evening.

Finally, she just grabbed her purse and keys and walked out of the door, unsure of where she was going, but needing to get out. She shook her head ruefully. This was probably exactly why everyone who knew she had the time off had reacted with such surprise when she'd told them she wasn't going anywhere.

It was a beautiful day—sunny and warm, but not hot. When she got to her car, she paused. What the hell did people who didn't work do all day? Shopping came to mind, and she seized upon the idea gratefully. Maybe she'd go to that fairly new open-air shopping centre and walk around, do some window shopping.

A few minutes later, she was driving with the windows down towards Cambridge Crossing, a huge and popular shopping area near her work. She hadn't spent a lot of time there before, but her co-workers spoke about going all the time, and she had been a handful of times when they'd had infrequent lunch or dinner functions around the holidays at some of the restaurants there.

As long as she was going to a place with nice stores, she should probably take a look at some new workout clothes. And casual stuff too. She was already starting to repeat herself, wearing the same things over and over, since she didn't have much depth to those sections of her wardrobe. Maybe a couple more summer dresses, she mused, thinking of how appreciative Adam had been of the two she had. He seemed to be a 'leg man'. Or maybe an 'ass man'… She was always catching him lifting his gaze from her lower half.

She giggled to herself for a moment, then sobered. Well, whatever turned him on, her parts obviously weren't exciting enough to make him lose control. Despite the admiring glances, he was so damn gentlemanly it was starting to give her a complex. They'd been seeing each other for weeks now and still hadn't done more than kiss. At this rate, she wouldn't be having sex before Christmas, much less before her sabbatical was up.

Yes, the shopping centre was the perfect place to spend today. It was time to turn up the heat. So he liked what he saw? Maybe it was time to show off a little bit more of it.

* * * *

Three exhausting hours later, she was several hundred dollars poorer and sitting on the outdoor patio of a café, sipping an iced tea while waiting for her lunch. Bags from a multitude of stores covered the other chairs around the table. She was going to have to make a trip to the car after this. She had actually been headed towards the parking structure when she'd passed the restaurant and realised just how hungry she was.

Adam had told her from the start that she'd definitely need to eat regular meals to fuel her revved up metabolism, and that was no joke. She was starving half the time now. Before, she would skip breakfast and fuel herself with coffee until lunch, pick at something light then, and eat most of her calories for the day after she was home in the evening. Now, the opposite was true. Breakfast was a necessity since she always woke up ravenous, as were snacks throughout the day, especially after workouts. So by the time dinner rolled around, she didn't seem to eat as much as she used to.

Whatever Adam was doing to her, she was already seeing results and, to her delight, she'd had to try on clothes a size less than she'd been wearing. That had made all the time spent in the dressing rooms today much more fun.

In some instances, she'd gone down two sizes, because, frankly, she'd always worn things a bit loose-fitting. Now that she had seduction on her mind, she wanted to show off her assets — pun intended. The short skirts, form-fitting pants and shorts she'd ended up buying made her feel very sexy and confident and she couldn't wait to show them off to Adam. She'd also splurged on some high-end workout clothing and found some good sports bras that didn't so much flatten as accentuate her modest bust.

Just in case he wasn't all about the lower half.

And her new swimsuits were ten times more flattering than her old one. A racer-style one-piece for workouts in the pool, and a halter-style bikini for trips to the beach.

She surveyed her bags with satisfaction, thinking she would look for shoes next.

"Victoria?"

The use of her full name in this setting caught her off guard. Turning sideways in her chair in the direction of the interior of the café, she nearly groaned at the sight of Terrence Michaels walking towards her. He was dressed as he usually did for work, so had probably just finished lunch and was heading back to the facility. Hopefully that meant he wouldn't have time to linger.

Even as she thought that, she knew it was a false hope. While a brilliant researcher, he was also a social butterfly and wasted a lot of time chit-chatting, at least that's how it seemed from Tori's perspective. That difference was only one of many reasons their brief relationship hadn't worked out.

"Pardon me, sir."

Terrence had stopped by Tori's chair, and at that he spun around, almost knocking Tori's lunch from the server's tray. Her quick reflexes and probably experience with dodging clueless customers had her moving back in time to save the club sandwich from becoming bird food.

"Oh, excuse me." Terrence stepped to the side to allow the server to place Tori's plate in front of her. Without asking, he began clearing some of her bags from the chair adjacent to her then sat down.

"Can I get you something, sir?"

"No thanks, I just ate. Wait... I'll have an iced tea. That looks good. No lemon."

"Certainly. Anything else I can bring you, miss?"

A bit put out that Terrence had just crashed her nice solo lunch and appeared to be settling in for a long stay, she shook her head at the waitress. "No, thank you."

As soon as she'd left, Tori met Terrence's interested smirk. "Shouldn't you be getting back to work?" she prompted.

"Probably," he replied cheerfully. "But I couldn't just leave you sitting here all by yourself."

"Yes, you could've. I was just fine alone." Tori turned her attention to her plate and began rearranging her sandwich, taking the extra slice of bread from the middle.

"Why don't you just ask them to make it without from the start? I swear, that's just like you. You never assert yourself."

Seriously? She tried to ignore her intruder and took a big bite of the club.

"I couldn't believe I saw you here. You should be off somewhere fun instead of hanging around wishing you were at work." The way he watched her, waiting for her to take the bait, finally got to her.

She swallowed and took a sip of her tea, then glared at Terrence. "I am *not* wishing I was at work. I'm shopping and having lunch."

"Yes you are. Right *by* work." Terrence glanced up as the server placed his tea in front of him then topped off Tori's from a pitcher. He began adding a couple of packets of sugar to his glass as he continued, "I mean, of all the places in the city to shop, you picked this one because…"

"Because I know where it is. I wanted to come to the stores here and it has nothing to do with work. And in case you'd forgotten, I live about fifteen minutes from here, so it's also the closest one to my home." She took another bite of her sandwich, figuring that the quicker she ate, the faster she could leave.

Part of her knew that Terrence was right, though she would rather shave her head than admit it to the smug man. A few weeks ago, she might have come here on the off-chance that she'd run into someone from her division and be able to catch up on what was happening at work. But now she had her goals and Adam…

Never assert myself, huh? If only you knew…

She ate another mouthful to keep herself from blurting out anything about her newfound outlook on life. Though she now counted him as a friend, Terrence could be a self-important blabbermouth and was a part of her past she wished she could undo.

"Okay, okay, don't get all upset. So what have you been doing with your time off? Besides a lot of shopping." He began to peek into the bags on the chair beside him.

"Do you mind?" She sighed. *Whatever.* What the hell had she ever seen in him? When he'd first joined her division, she had been given the task of orienting him to the facility and mentoring him while he learnt their procedures and standards. His outgoing personality had seemed charming at first, and he was attractive, with closely cut, curly blond hair and bright blue eyes behind his rimless glasses. He was tall and thin and dressed nicely, and he'd teased and prodded Tori until she'd agreed to go out with him.

They'd had a quasi-relationship away from work for a couple of months. Inevitably, she'd become disenchanted with his nosy, opinionated, loud persona, while he'd begun nagging her about how frigid and uptight she was. Things had been awkward in bed and even more awkward at work. She'd finally ended it, and their friendship and working relationship was much the better for it. Still, even though they got along decently, she could only take so much of him before she went into avoidance mode. To that end, she polished off the first half of the sandwich.

"So you never answered me. I'm seeing workout clothes but you've never really exercised before. Did you join a gym?" He looked her up and down with narrowed eyes. "I guess you are looking pretty decent."

"Thanks," she replied drily. "I have a personal trainer at Del Sol."

"Ooh, fancy," he teased. "Spending the big bucks, are you? Well, it's about time. You aren't getting any younger. I would go there, but I don't really need to work out." He patted his abdomen.

Tori repressed a snort. She knew what was under his shirt, and, while trim, it wasn't exactly the fit musculature she was now used to seeing with Adam. Though she honestly didn't care what Terrence did, she still felt compelled to say, "Everyone should work out, if only to improve their fitness and heart health. And you won't stay thin forever if you don't start doing something about it. *You* aren't exactly getting any younger either."

"Bitch," he shot back without heat, though his brow puckered and he ran a hand over his belly.

"Jerk," she returned. They laughed together.

"We've missed you at work. I'll bet you can't wait until September." Terrence leant back in his chair then pulled out his phone when a ping was heard. "Sorry, just a sec," he offered.

Tori thought about that for a few minutes while she took advantage of his distraction to finish her lunch, and found that while part of her would be glad to return to work, she was beginning to realise that she'd let her life revolve around it for far too long, that there were so many other things to enjoy.

She wondered if she hadn't met Adam that day, if she would have had the same thought. If she was being honest with herself, she'd have to say no. And that was a bit scary, to think that she'd have taken the same approach to her enforced sabbatical as she did to her work and kept a narrow focus rather than open herself up to new, exciting possibilities.

Even the way she'd been approaching her sabbatical goals was way too rigid. She grimaced. Treating them like an experiment? She should just let go and enjoy, and let what would happen, happen.

Let go? It was a very foreign concept and a frightening one.

Take a chance. Adam will catch you.

More terrifying than letting go, though, was the idea that she could become so dependent on having someone in her life, with no guarantee that he'd be around for the long run. And why would he be? He was so much younger than her. Why would he want more than whatever sort of fling this was with her? They hadn't made any promises to each other, of course. For all she knew, he just enjoyed her company, or maybe he saw her as a 'project' as far as getting her fit and being a sort of tour guide for her vacation.

Terrence put his phone back in his pocket and smiled at Tori. "Sorry, Victoria, have to run. It was great seeing you. Don't be a stranger. Let's have lunch for real sometime, okay?"

He stood and pulled out a five and tossed it on the table, then leaned over and pecked her on the cheek. With a last goodbye and admonition to call him, he walked out of the iron-fenced off area and joined the throngs moving along the sidewalk.

Tori watched him until he was out of sight. A bit symbolic that here she'd been confronted with a representation of both her all-consuming work life and her dysfunctional sex life, and had no desire to go back to either one as she had been. Being Victoria was a part of her past. The lack of a social life, the sensible clothes, the unhealthy workload and lifestyle—all of that was over. She knew the changes she was making this summer would stick with her.

They just had to.

Tori smiled as she decided to sit for a while longer and linger over her tea.

Chapter Six

The doorbell pealed. Adam glanced around his apartment one last time to make sure he hadn't forgotten anything on his way to answer the door. They'd always spent their time together either at Tori's or the club or met elsewhere. This was the first time Tori had been to his place and, though it wasn't much, he wanted to make a decent impression.

He swung it open, a greeting for Tori still on his lips as he froze at the sight of her tight derrière pointed in his direction, shown off by a short skirt he hadn't seen before that had risen almost to the point of indecency. In addition to her purse, she had a bag over one shoulder that he recognised from training and he was glad that she'd taken his advice and brought swimwear. Right now, though, she had her weight on one foot and was bent over, doing something to her sandal. She muttered a swear word and he smiled.

"Tori, you okay?"

"Oh!" She teetered and he caught her by the arm to help her balance. "Stupid new shoes. I got something in between the sole and my foot."

"Ouch," he commiserated then stooped to catch her behind the legs and shoulders and pick her up.

Tori gasped and instinctively clutched at him as he settled her in his arms and turned to carry her inside.

"Can you get the door?" he asked and moved so that she could catch the door handle and swing it shut. "Thanks." He proceeded into the living room and set her down on the couch.

"Wow, um, thanks. It's a bit early on to be carrying me across the threshold, isn't it?"

Adam laughed and knelt at her feet. He began to undo the buckle of her sandal, noticing the new bright pink pedicure she was sporting. "Nice pedi," he commented as he worked the shoe off. Sure enough, a sharp-looking piece of gravel fell to the floor.

"Yes, well… I bought the new shoes yesterday and noticed that most of the other women I saw had theirs done, and I saw a place, so…" She shrugged and raised an eyebrow at him. "You noticed? Somehow that doesn't seem like a guy thing."

"I notice everything about you." He lifted her foot until he could lightly kiss her toes. "I like it." He replaced the sandal on her foot and fastened it, unable to resist sliding his hand along her smooth calf afterwards.

"Thanks." Her voice was a bit breathless and she didn't move away from his touch. If anything, she scooted a bit closer until he was framed by her legs on either side of him.

He was starting to feel the effects of her proximity and he shifted to accommodate his semi-erection. "This is getting to be a thing with us. Me on my knees in front of you." He could think of something else he'd love to do to her while on his knees.

Her lips parted and she ran her tongue over the lower one.

He could barely keep back a groan as he continued to run his hands farther up her legs to the silky backs of her knees. "I missed you yesterday. Did you have a good day?"

"Yes," she answered, wriggling a bit and bringing her legs closer together until she'd effectively trapped Adam in place. Not that it was a hardship being there. Well, maybe that was the wrong way to look at it, because something was hard…

"What did you do all day?" he asked, telling himself he could move away any time now.

She smiled, her gaze locked on his. "Shopped." She punctuated the succinct answer with a slight squeeze of her knees against his sides.

Oh, she was killing him.

"And what did you buy?"

"All sorts of sexy new clothes…from the skin out…for every occasion."

"From the skin out, huh?"

"Yep. Wanna preview?" she teased. "A quick sneak peek?" She ran her fingers under the hem of her skirt, which was already high enough on her thighs that it was barely keeping whatever lay under it covered.

Before he could answer or react, she quickly lifted the hem, flashing him a view of something dark blue and lacy, before dropping it back in place and scooting up on the couch. She giggled as she primly closed her thighs and sat to the side with her feet up on the cushions beside her.

He rose to his feet and towered over her. "Hey, no shoes on the couch." Two could play at this game. Grasping her by the ankles, he gave a gentle tug that sent her off balance and sliding onto one elbow. She gasped with laughter as she tried to regain her poise and also keep her skirt from riding up. He was having none of that. He quickly undid the first sandal then removed it and tossed it aside, followed by the other.

"And I didn't get a very good look. I think I need another peek."

She half-heartedly scrambled to try to get away, but he soon had her flat on her back and breathless with laughter as he wedged himself between her legs and knelt on the couch.

"Hmm, where were we?" He raked her up and down with his gaze. She stopped chuckling and swallowed, though he was glad to see that a smile still teased at the corners of her mouth. "Oh, yes, I think we were right about here." He slid his hands up her outer legs to her thighs and stopped right at the askew hem. It was ruched up almost to her hip on the right side.

Adam slid his hand farther up until he was pushing the material of the skirt up her hip with it...and up and up. His eyebrows rose. He finally got to a midnight blue spaghetti strap about even with her hip bone.

He looked from her exposed hip with the sexy, barely there lingerie to her heated gaze.

"Very nice." His voice was a bit hoarse. He reminded himself of his vow to not become intimate with her until they'd passed her deadline. This time his groan was aloud. There was no way he was going to make it until September with her bringing out the big guns by making trips to the lingerie store.

Damn it.

Of course, he justified to himself, there were degrees to everything. Maybe withholding *all* sex was unrealistic...

"So you like them?"

He followed the strap with his finger to where it met a miniscule patch of lace then trailed down to the warm crease of her inner leg.

"What I can see of them, yes."

"Do you need a better look to be sure?"

While he was loving Tori's increased confidence and pride, it was wreaking havoc with his restraint. From the attraction burning between them to the teasing thus far—which was basically the hottest non-contact foreplay he'd ever experienced—he could easily see this concluding with him pressing her into the cushions as he sank deep into the heat of her, making long, slow love to her.

It would be so much easier to let things take their natural course. But the thought of this encounter being written dispassionately into her notebook, her goal checked off as complete, was like a dash of cold water. He didn't want what he seemed to be building with Tori to end when her holiday was over. Adam wasn't a relationship expert by any means, but he hoped that the longer he could draw things out, building their anticipation, the more time they'd have to grow close in other ways. Then maybe she'd see him as more than a means to an end, more than an affair.

He made his living with his body, so he knew that it was probably his best trait, but he didn't want to be just a hot bod and a good fuck. He was getting too old for hook-ups and casual dating. He wanted to forge something lasting with someone he enjoyed spending time with, a woman he enjoyed talking to and missed when she was gone. Like he did with Tori.

And he wanted her to feel that way about him. God, he wanted that—just as much, if not more than the physical side of things. Adam had a feeling that when they did finally have sex it would blow anything he'd previously done out of the water. The chemistry between them had been sizzling from the start.

He realised that Tori was now frowning slightly and he mentally backtracked to where they'd left off. Decision time. Did he back off, or change direction?

"I'd love a closer look." The words came out of his mouth almost before he had thought them, making his decision for him.

Desire warred with uncertainty in her eyes, and Adam smiled reassuringly. Perhaps she'd reached the limits of her forwardness for today. It made it easier for him to clamp down on his own libido in favour of pleasing her.

Time for an old-fashioned make-out session. Adult-style.

His feet were already bare to match hers. He stripped off his shirt and watched as her gaze went straight to his chest. Suddenly he had new motivation to keep him focused during his workouts, if only to always be able to warrant the admiration in her gaze. She reached out then hesitated.

Not wanting her to start second-guessing herself, he grasped her hand and pulled it towards his chest as he knee-walked closer to her. He pressed her hand to the centre of his torso, silently encouraging her exploration, then released her. She kept it in place then ran it up over his left pec and down across his pebbling nipple. The light touch sent a jolt straight to his cock. She trailed her fingertips down his abs then ran her index finger back up the centre to where she'd started.

"You're amazing," she whispered and met his gaze directly.

For a few moments, he looked his fill at the sight of her lying on his couch, auburn hair spread beneath her, eyes almost the same reddish hue locked on his, warm with desire. "So are you," he returned and bent to kiss her.

She lifted slightly to meet him, showing that she wanted the connection as badly as he did at that moment. Her lips moved against his, prompting his deepening the kiss while he curved his hand under the back of her neck to tangle into her hair.

He stroked his tongue between her lips as he settled his chest lightly against hers. Their breath mingled as they tasted deeply of each other. Tori brought her hands up to slide into Adam's, with gentle tugs to increase the slant and deepen the kiss even further. They clung to each other, using their lips and hands to explore.

Adam was rock hard and panting by the time they parted and he trailed his lips down her neck. Never before had he been so affected by this sort of teasing play. She arched back, exposing her throat and he obliged by nipping and sucking lightly down to the sweet spot where neck and shoulder came together. He dipped his tongue into the divot at her throat then nibbled along her collarbone. Before moving any farther down, he lifted his head to ascertain her comfort level.

Seeing only heat in her gaze, her kiss-swollen lips parted to breathe, he sat back and pulled her upright. He gave her a wink before grasping the hem of her shirt. "This okay?"

"More than okay," came the immediate and reassuring answer.

Adam slowly lifted her knitted shirt until it was just under her breasts, then stopped, lowering his head to kiss lightly at her ribs. He nuzzled the material upwards accompanied by long licks along her abdomen.

With a frustrated sound, Tori batted him away and grabbed her shirt, whipping it up and over her head before sending it sailing across the room. Then she reclined back on her elbows on the couch in just her short skirt and a dark blue, lacy bra that barely covered her areolae.

She arched an eyebrow and smirked. "So, is this a close enough look for you? What do you think?"

Chapter Seven

Tori couldn't believe she'd just done that, but there was something extremely empowering about how Adam was so intent upon her every move. She'd wanted to take a more active role and surprise him, and by the looks of it, she'd succeeded.

"What do I think?" He reached a finger out and traced the edge of the lace over her breast, sending a shiver through her. Her nipple puckered as though reaching for his touch. The tightness coiled in her breast as her skin seemed to anticipate the contact.

"About the view."

Adam, the tease, didn't follow up on the promise, instead tickling a path along the slope of her other breast until it was similarly stirred.

"Adam..." He was driving her nuts with his deliberateness. She wished she could just tackle him and...

Hmm...

She levered herself up, narrowly avoiding a collision, to a sitting position on the couch.

Looking startled then worried, Adam asked, "Everything okay?"

"No." Planting both hands on his bare chest and pushing, she managed to get him off balance, then launched herself at him. He ended up on the floor beneath her as she straddled him. His hands automatically came up to cup her hips. She braced her hands on the floor to either side of his head and leaned over him to whisper in his ear, "You are making me crazy."

His gaze dipped to her cleavage and a groan escaped him. "Very mutual."

When she glanced down, she could plainly see her nipples from her vantage point. Making no move to adjust her bra, she smiled and shimmied up his torso a bit until she was nearly breast to mouth over him.

"Fuck it," he muttered and brought his hands up from her hips to hook a finger on each cup and pull down until her breasts had both popped completely free of the material. He tucked the bra underneath them so they were supported and helped forward.

Adam cupped one in his large hand as he lifted his head the small fraction he needed to draw her peak into the warmth of his mouth. The other hand he ran up her back, holding her close to him so she couldn't pull away. Not that she wanted to. Ever.

"Oh God..." She arched even closer as he suckled her to an even more pronounced point then lightly used his teeth to run along the base of her nipple. After one last long suck, he pulled off with a pop and moved to the other side, laving and nipping until she was squirming with need.

Adam slid the hand that had been cupping her breast down her bare side to the waistband of her skirt then around to the small of her back. A cool waft of air signalled that her skirt was being moved out of the way. Then his questing, warm hand was cupping her bare ass, tracing the crease, and she knew the moment he realised she was wearing a thong…

The world spun as he rolled and changed their positions so he was cradled in between her thighs. The roughness of his khaki shorts pressed against the soft skin of her inner thighs, and she wished she was a genie and could just blink their clothes away. Not that there was much on her part. The lace thong she'd purchased was the only thing between her pussy and his shorts, and it was so thin as to be barely a token.

He pulled away and she protested wordlessly but it was only to return his attention to her breasts. "Beautiful," he murmured against her skin.

Reaching down with the intent to tug him up so his weight was on her once again, she got sidetracked first by the feel of his muscular shoulders beneath her hands, then she threaded her fingers through his hair. God, his mouth on her… But her core was on fire and she wanted—needed—him back against her. She gave his hair a tug at the same time as she wrapped her legs around his hips and used some of her newfound strength to attempt to move him in the right direction.

"Beautiful…and bossy." He laughed down at her but acceded to her efforts and moved up so he was once again nestled against her. Oh bliss… He was braced up on his elbows to either side of her head to keep most of his weight off her chest, but she could feel the ridge of his erection pressed firmly to her, right where she needed the counter-pressure.

She rocked up against him, and his head went back, exposing his corded neck. She strained upwards to try to give it a lick but couldn't quite reach. His neck looked just a touch stubbly and she could almost taste the salt...

He dropped his head back down to rest against her temple, curled around her and she got her chance, dragging her tongue across his Adam's apple. A bit salty, yes, and the texture and flavour together were wholly masculine and an amazing treat for her senses.

The groan that went through him vibrated against her lips and she smiled. They moved together with a rhythm that approximated deep, slow sex. His hard cock dragged over her swollen clit through their clothes in just the right way. He irregularly thumbed her peak, keeping it taut, while his other hand supported her head. She moved her head towards him and he captured her mouth in a tender, questing kiss. The whole of it was almost too much. Seldom had she been able to climax with another person in her life, but just from this make-out session, she hovered on the edge. How amazing would actual sex be?

That thought had her gasping into his mouth. Adam responded by rotating his hips and the change in motion caught her clit in the just the right way to send her over the precipice. A long moan came from deep within her as she arched, trying to get as close to him as humanly possible. With one last tweak of her breast, he moved his hand under her ass to help her press against him, and she rode out the waves of sensation.

As she came back to herself, she noticed they were both damp with perspiration, their skin clinging together. Far from it being a turn-off, it felt utterly intimate and right. But... Adam hadn't...

He shifted then onto his side and turned her so that he was spooned up behind her.

How to bring it up? "Adam, don't you want to...?"

A huff of air shifted the hair along her warm scalp. "Of course I want to, but it's not going to kill me to wait. Blue balls aren't terminal," he joked. "It was amazing to watch you climax, and that's enough for me for this evening."

Her cheeks were flaming and she was glad in a way that they weren't having this conversation face to face. "But if you want to and I want you to... I guess I don't understand."

He traced random circles on her bare abdomen with his fingers, sending shivers almost like aftershocks through her. "Anticipation makes everything sweeter. We don't have any reason to race to the finish line and cross everything off tonight... Do we?"

Her notebooks popped into her mind and a twinge of guilt hit her. "Of course not," she replied—and she meant that. For the first time, she wondered whether she wasn't being unfair by targeting Adam, using him to reach a personal goal. No, she argued with herself, she wasn't *using* him. Looking back on it, it had stopped being about that after their first date. That first night she had come to know him, and she really liked what made Adam who he was—far more than a pretty face, he was a beautiful man inside and out. If only he wasn't so damn young...

"Something on your mind? I hope you enjoyed what we did. You seem lost in thought." He gave her a squeeze from behind and she could feel that he was still at least partially hard against her nearly bare ass. He had never even taken his shorts off.

She shook her head. "No. Just feeling a bit guilty that I... Well, you know. And you didn't get anything out of it."

He had her on her back faster than she could blink. "Oh, trust me, Tori. I got a great deal of enjoyment out of seeing you come apart in my arms." He pressed a firm but quick kiss to her lips then rose to his knees. His gaze traced her and she became aware that her breasts were still exposed from her bra and her skirt was up around her waist.

It was a bit embarrassing, but more than that she had to laugh. "It's like we're a couple of teenagers or something, making out on the couch with our clothes still on." She sat up and adjusted her bra and smoothed down her skirt as best she could. She could feel the fibres of the carpet under her ass. She'd been a bit leery of trying a thong, thinking it might be uncomfortable, but it wasn't bad at all. She'd sort of forgotten it was there, and the reaction Adam had had to discovering it had made it so worth all the time she'd spent trying on lingerie and looking at her forty-something body in the mirror of the extremely well-lit dressing room.

At least the working out she'd been doing had started to pay off in the end...*her* end. She giggled at the double entendre.

"Now that's what I like to hear." Adam grinned at her, stood and held his hands down to her. She clasped them and he levered her to her feet then pulled her into a hug. Tori was beginning to cool down now and feel a bit sticky. She couldn't help a grimace as their bare torsos separated.

"Yeah, I agree." He nodded. "I'm thinking we go for that dip in the complex pool before dinner. I'm planning to grill anyway, and it's warm enough that we could just stay in our suits while we cook and eat. Kind of like being in Hawaii."

"Hawaii. I've always wanted to go there," Tori confessed. She'd never been, but a lot of her co-workers took annual trips there.

Adam stared at her with an odd expression. "You've never been to Hawaii? It's only a five-hour flight from here."

She squirmed a bit. "Yes, I know. I told you I don't get out much." She was irritated, but more with herself than him. She shrugged, trying not to get defensive. "I've just never taken many vacations, and I'm not sure who I'd go with anyway."

Adam put a soothing hand on her shoulder and walked with her towards where they'd dropped her bags earlier. "I didn't mean that, necessarily. I just thought that since you'd grown up in California you might have gone with your family at some point."

She snickered at the image of her parents in Hawaii. "That's just funny. I'm sorry. No, they're not the tropical holiday types. My mom is way more of a redhead than I am and she's terrified of the sun...and of anything out of the ordinary routine, for that matter. And when Dad's not at work, he's glued to his laptop, tinkering with his experiments. They're pretty much homebodies." She shrugged again, knowing that she'd probably inherited the worst possible combination of traits from both parents. The non-adventurous part of her mom and the workaholic part of her dad.

Adam handed her shirt, purse and bag with her suit in it to her. "No siblings?"

"No, just me." She looked at him curiously. "You?"

"God, yes. Two of each, but we're all over the country. We all try to get together — as many of us as possible, anyway — at least once or twice a year, usually in the summer somewhere fun, then at Dad's or my oldest sister Becky's for one of the holidays."

"That sounds like fun," she said wistfully. She had no idea what it would be like having that many people around while growing up. She thought about her quiet upbringing, and guessed that Adam's would have been completely different.

"It was, but look at how well you turned out. I'm sure yours was good too."

She turned to him, grateful for his attempts to set her at ease. "Thank you." She rose on tiptoe to peck him on the cheek. "Okay, I'm going to get changed, and we can go pretend like we're in the islands."

Adam smiled at her then indicated the hallway off the living room. "You can change in the bedroom or the bathroom, up to you." He snorted self-deprecatingly. "I'd give you the grand tour, but it's hard to get lost in an apartment this small."

"It's very nice, even if it's not big," she said truthfully. "Sometimes I wish I was in one more this size again, especially on cleaning days. But I bought it mostly for the proximity to the beach, that and the fact my co-worker had the inside scoop on how low the seller would go. Ex-boyfriend," she explained.

"That was nice of her."

"Him, actually." Tori laughed at Adam's expression of chagrin.

"Oops. That's what I get for assuming. Sorry. That was nice of *him*."

"Yes, it was, and until then—about five years ago—I was in an apartment almost exactly this size."

"All right, well if you use the bathroom, I'll get changed too and I'll meet you on the patio for our trip to paradise," he teased.

She smiled, loving their camaraderie.

And she couldn't wait to get his reaction when she showed him her new swimsuit.

Chapter Eight

Tori could already feel the exertion of the day, the uncertainty and stress of her confusion over the situation with Adam, sloughing off as she was led at a measured, deliberate pace through the inner sanctum of the spa. Even though it was in the same building as the gym, the two areas seemed worlds apart.

Pausing outside the last door on the left side of the corridor, the small, older woman indicated silently that Tori should precede her into the room.

The muted, warm lighting was a balm to her over-sensitised eyes, which still spent more time than they should staring at the screen of her computer, e-reader or phone. The soothing aromatic combinations of scents — she thought she recognised rosemary? — made breathing deeply noticeable and rewarding. Even the temperature was ideal. Entering an atmosphere like this sent a signal to her muscles and posture to give it up and relax already. More than an indulgence, this massage session would be a true test of her ability to relax. She was hopeful that, if it proved so, she could continue to make regular visits even after she returned to work.

The attendant poured a glass of water. She instructed Tori to hang up her wrap and robe and lie face down under the sheet on the massage table, before quietly leaving. This was her first ever visit to a spa, and so far she'd found the experience to be particularly efficient and tranquil. Adam had suggested that she give herself some extra time before her appointment to indulge in the steam room, and she was glad he had. Depending on how she felt afterwards, there was also a hot tub to soak in before returning to the shower area. The whole experience, coupled with the tea and snacks in the lush, peaceful lounge, turned a simple ninety-minute massage into a nearly three-hour escape.

Today, instead of just a straightforward massage, she had also elected to receive a hot wrap treatment. With all of the impending changes in her life, she had paradoxically needed something even more different to shake up her routine. Since Adam was usually the one who came up with ideas, she'd been fairly proud of herself that she'd thought of a spa visit on her own. So she'd asked Adam whether the gym spa was worth looking into, and he'd seemed very pleased at her interest. He'd immediately pulled up the list of services for her. She had been drawn to the wrap treatment she'd selected, which evidently shortened the initial massage to leave time for a rejuvenating, hot lemongrass and eucalyptus wrap, then was finished with a shea butter massage and Vichy shower. If it was half as good as it sounded, it would be heavenly.

Shrugging off her soft robe and slipping from the one-size-fits-all terry wrap and nubby spa sandals, Tori took a quick, obligatory sip of the water before climbing up onto the table, settling on her front as directed. She threw the sheet haphazardly over her bare ass, and spent a great deal of fruitless effort trying to cover herself before giving up. She wasn't the least bit chilly, and it was a pain to try to spread it out behind her back. Besides, she had a feeling that the masseur or masseuse would end up arranging it the way they liked it.

Giving her neck a roll, she made sure she was adjusted so that her face hit the hole in the table comfortably, then settled in to wait for her practitioner.

The soft, instrumental music they'd chosen to play was peaceful at the moment, but it was the kind of flutey, New Age music that only really worked as background music in places like this. Tori smiled wryly as she recalled the CD Terrance had given her as a gift after a trip years ago—he had spontaneously purchased the music from a similar spa. She had no idea where the thing even was anymore—she'd played it once in naïve hopes of recreating the spa atmosphere he'd described at home. Out of context, it had bugged the hell out of her after only a track or two.

The door opened and closed and she could sense a presence approaching the table. A deep, resonant voice quietly broke the stillness.

"Hi. Tori?" There was a pause, and just before she spoke up to confirm, he continued, "I'm Steve, and I'll be taking care of you this evening." A bit of movement and she grinned down at the floor as she felt Steve, as she'd predicted, wasting no time in adjusting the sheet. It billowed slightly then settled so it covered her whole body from neck to foot. A couple of quiet sounds from the counter area were followed by his settling a very warm towel over the sheet, reaching from her nape to the small of her back.

"We'll begin with some aromatherapy. I'll be holding three different scents for you to sample. Just let me know if you prefer the first, second or third. Make sure to take deep, cleansing breaths between each choice."

Number two something-or-other was Tori's undisputed choice, not that she would remember the name later on, so she just tuned out the descriptions and told him her preference when he asked. The sudden, strong scent enveloped her, slamming her into an expectant headspace and she could feel the last remnants of the real world slip away.

Minutes ticked by without anything happening, and Tori slowly began to come back out of her inwardly focused state to wonder what Steve was doing.

Just as she was about to lift her head to look around, a slight movement off to her left settled her nerves. Now that she knew where he was, she relaxed and waited for whatever would happen next.

Another hot towel, warm almost to the point of discomfort, was placed on the back of her neck. She shifted a bit.

"Too warm?" he asked.

"Almost, but it's fine," she answered. Still, he lifted the towel away and did something swishy-sounding to her right. It was replaced and to her relief felt much less warm.

"Better?"

"Definitely, thank you." She opened her eyes but couldn't see anything more interesting than the floor, so she closed them again.

A hand touched her back with light pressure that gradually increased, then the other was added. They just rested there, giving her a chance to get used to the feel. Steve began to rub her back in long strokes through the covering for a few minutes, then pulled the sheet down and folded it at the base of her spine, leaving her legs covered.

As he added a warmed oil to her skin and used it to smooth, rub and knead, she gave herself over to the wonderfully relaxing sensation. She lay there for an unknown amount of time, and he would periodically bare a section of her body after covering what he'd previously been working on, until she had been massaged all over and was melting into the table.

She realised that she was inexplicably becoming aroused. It was a slow burn, nothing like what she felt with Adam, of course, but there nonetheless. It was a bit of an eye-opener to have a physical response to someone else, and she wasn't exactly sure how to mentally process that.

"Okay, I'm going to hold the sheet up and I want you to turn away from me so that you're lying on your back. Go ahead and turn when you're ready."

Tori did as she had been instructed, opening her eyes and blinking even in the soft light. She noted that Steve was, as he'd said, holding the sheet up so she had privacy, even though she found to her surprise she wouldn't have been too terribly upset for him to have seen her. After all, he did this for a living and she wasn't in terrible shape thanks to Adam...

Steve lowered the sheet and Tori gasped then started laughing. *Steve, ha!*

"Adam! What are you doing in here?"

He grinned at her then lifted an eyebrow. "Did you think I'd let just anyone give you your first real massage?"

She returned his smile and relaxed even more now that she knew her body had been reacting more appropriately than her conscious mind had known. "You seem to know what you're doing."

"I'm a licensed massage therapist, too. Actually did this while working my way through school." He moved to stand at her head and gathered her hair back out of the way then began to give her a facial massage that had her eyes drifting shut again.

Tori did the best she could to keep herself from squirming as he continued the massage down her neck to her shoulders and upper chest. She swore he was just missing her nipples by an inch each time he ran his hands over her pecs. They stiffened against the sheet covering them and she thought she heard a masculine chuckle but didn't want to open her eyes to see if he was watching her breasts betray her arousal.

Adam worked her arms from the shoulders down to her fingers, then moved to her side and did something complicated with the sheet so her hip was bared but all the interesting parts were still covered. She loved how seriously he was taking his massage duties, and smiled to herself thinking about how gentlemanly he was, even when she wished he'd be a bit naughtier.

A spike of want hit her low, making her pussy throb, and his hands slowly but firmly running along her flank didn't help.

"Adam…" she moaned.

"Tori, I can't in here."

"Can't what?" she asked, even though she knew. Damn him.

Adam spoke in a low, intimate tone. "I can't do to you what you're aching for. It goes against my professional standards and licensing." He bent to whisper in her ear. "But nothing says you can't do it yourself."

"Oh God," she breathed. Her hand went straight under the sheet to her needy core without her even willing it. Adam rearranged the sheet again so that it covered her from the neck down, and moved to the foot of the table.

As she met his heated gaze, she frantically worked at her clit and slick folds, needing only a few short minutes of friction to bring her close to the edge. Adam's expression bounced between pained and encouraging as he slicked his hands with lotion and began to give her a foot massage.

"God, Adam... Oh my God."

His hands on her feet and his position of visually being between her legs while she masturbated there in the spa room all became too much for her to take. He slid his hands up her calf then back down before switching to give his attention to her other foot.

"You're so beautiful," he said hoarsely and that sign of his own arousal sent her wheeling into an intense orgasm, arching her head back then lifting her head to stare at Adam before dropping back to the table, sated and boneless.

Adam quickly wrapped up his foot massage and walked over to give her a peck on the temple.

"I'll have the masseuse you were originally booked with come in to do your wrap in about ten minutes, okay, hon?"

Tori blinked open her eyes, which she hadn't even realised she'd closed. "Masseuse?"

Adam smiled and stroked her hair. "Enjoy," he murmured then touched her cheek tenderly before walking to the door.

When will that man ever stop surprising me? Not that I want him to.

Chapter Nine

"I can't believe we're doing this."

It must've been the hundredth time Tori had said that in the past thirty-six hours or so, and Adam still smiled every time he heard it.

He grasped her hand where it was resting on the armrest between their seats and looked past her out of the plane's window. They were on their final descent and could see the islands now, breaking up the vast continuity of the Pacific Ocean they'd been flying over for several hours.

The cabin crew had come through and collected their drink cups a few minutes earlier, so Adam put his tray table up then watched Tori's profile as she stared out of the window.

When they'd talked a couple of weeks previously about how she'd never been to Hawaii, the longing in her voice had struck a chord in Adam. Tori loved being on the small section of beach just blocks from her condo and walked there almost daily. But to think she'd never experienced the beautiful exotic difference of Hawaii when it was so easy to get there had seemed a shame to Adam.

So he'd started looking into planning a trip and had found that, since it was summer, it was fairly inexpensive to fly there and vacation rentals were plentiful. Since he made his own schedule, he'd simply picked the five-day stretch that had the least number of bookings, then arranged for another of the trainers to cover his slots.

He hadn't been sure how Tori would take it— planning a vacation without her knowledge—but he'd gone ahead and booked their flights and the rental in a small but nice condo complex in the middle of Maui. Then he'd printed out the brochure and flight information and given it to her in an envelope over dinner the night before last.

Waiting for her to look at the papers and react had been one of the longest waits of his life, but when she'd looked up with happy tears in her eyes and a huge smile for him, he'd finally relaxed and enjoyed the success of his surprise.

At least until she'd jumped to her feet in a panic about what to pack and the fact that the flight was only a day and a half away.

He'd tried to assure her that less was more, and that a carry-on would be plenty for what they'd need for their short stay, especially since they'd be living in casual wear and swimsuits the whole time. And, he'd added, it wasn't like they were going on safari. They could shop there, and would be making a stop before checking in, anyway, for sunscreen and food supplies so they could cook and grill out at the condo.

She'd finally pared it down to the small floral rolling bag she'd shopped for yesterday afternoon, so between that and Adam's duffle bag, they wouldn't need to go to baggage claim.

They touched down at Kahului and finally got to the gate. When they deplaned and headed for the rental car counter, Adam enjoyed watching Tori's astonishment.

"It's all open." She gestured around. "What happens when it rains?"

"Honestly, I'm not sure. I've never had it rain when I've been here. But I'm sure they've designed it so that it works for them."

"Look at the colours, the beautiful flowers. Oh, Adam, this is amazing."

"And we're not even out of the airport yet. Just wait."

They got their car with a minimum of fuss and were on their way. Tori laughed that they went to the same chain grocery store that she shopped at while at home. Less than an hour after their plane had touched down, they were opening the door to the ground-level condo Adam had reserved.

It had white wicker furniture and was light and airy, with two bedrooms and bathrooms and a lanai from which you could walk right to both the pool and the beach. It also had a kitchen and a laundry—all of the comforts of home. It was an older complex but had obviously been renovated, and most of all it was on a small section of sand beach between the harbour and a wildlife refuge, so the beach was nearly empty but for a few couples strolling who were probably staying at the same complex. Much better than some of the huge hotels and resorts, in Adam's opinion.

"Thank you for this." Tori wrapped her arms around him where they were standing by the screen door to the lanai. She squeezed him tightly then lifted her lips for a kiss. He met her halfway and they shared a long, leisurely kiss there in the light island breeze. It was such a pleasure to do something for Tori that she wouldn't have done for herself.

He took one last taste then pulled away. "Okay, time to get into uniform. It's against the law to wear clothes in paradise. You brought the red polka dot suit, right?" He waggled his eyebrows at her and, as he'd predicted, she blushed. He loved her new bikini she'd worn to his apartment swimming a couple of weeks ago—so much so that he'd made a point of mentioning it almost daily since then.

As much as he loved it, he'd suggested that it would be practical to have a second suit along. She hadn't mentioned whether she'd bought one, but he knew she'd gone shopping for a while yesterday, longer than it would have taken just to buy a suitcase, so he had a suspicion that she had.

They walked back through the living area and stood there looking at the two bedrooms. They hadn't discussed sleeping arrangements, but Adam hadn't wanted to presume, so he'd made sure the condo he'd booked had two rooms. It had obviously been set up for a family. The master bedroom had a king-sized bed with a fluffy white comforter and a window that overlooked the pool and beach. It had a big en suite bathroom with a walk-in shower. The other bedroom had a double and a twin, both beds with matching red and blue striped coverlets, and a bathroom with a tub.

Without asking, he picked up her suitcase and took it into the master bedroom, leaving his duffle in the entryway. He set her bag on the dresser, turned around and froze.

Tori was putting his duffle bag on the suitcase rack by the closet.

Still, he tried. "I don't mind sleeping in the kids' room."

Tori laughed and walked towards him. "It is a kids' room, isn't it? No. I think we can share the king just fine. Besides, this room is much more romantic." She slid her arms around his waist.

He embraced her in return and pressed a kiss to the top of her head. He loved how she fitted perfectly against him when they hugged. "It is, isn't it?"

"Yes, and you have to be the most romantic guy in the world to do this. Seriously, Adam, I know I've probably said it a million times already, but this is the nicest thing anyone has ever done for me. Thank you."

His cheeks warmed under her intense gaze. "You're welcome. You deserve it." He just *had* to make it clear to her by the end of summer that they deserved a chance to try for something long term. There was too much at stake. His heart contracted at the thought of losing the woman in his arms and he cleared his throat. "So. Pool or beach? And would you like to eat in tonight or go out?"

* * * *

They ended up spending the remainder of the day walking on the beach, swimming, lounging on the lanai and by the pool. Then Tori fixed a small pitcher of margaritas and they visited with other guests and tenants at the communal grill as Adam grilled chicken breast skewers to have with their steamed rice and broccolini — a simple dish they ate outside and followed up with fresh pineapple shared by one of their neighbours.

"Come on, let's take a stroll," Adam whispered in her ear as they finished putting the kitchen to rights. His breath sent a shiver through her and she nodded.

"Let me grab a sweater."

They walked the short distance across the lawn to the sand then started meandering up the beach in the direction of the refuge, carrying their sandals. Earlier the waning light had been beautiful on the water, with the palm trees and Haleakalā in the distance. She'd taken several pictures on her phone and had sent one to her mom's email.

Adam took her hands in his and she smiled mostly to herself. What a romantic trip this had been, and it was only the first day. She wondered if tonight would be the night that they would finally make love. It seemed fitting somehow. The whole place was magical and serene and she could definitely see why people continued to come back to the islands time after time. She was already wondering how much it would be to purchase one of the condos in their complex. It was a mix of year-round owners and short-term tourists, and it was very low-key and nice...

What on earth was she thinking? Once she went back to work, she would have as little time as ever, and popping over to Hawaii just wasn't feasible or realistic. She might be older, but she wasn't retired yet.

She laughed out loud, thinking that she probably wasn't the first visitor to have fallen under the spell of the islands.

"Share?" Adam asked, rubbing her hand with his thumb.

Tori leaned against his upper arm. "I was just thinking about buying a condo here." Adam started laughing too. "Yes, I know. I was telling myself that it was a bit premature to think about retiring to Hawaii, even for someone my age."

"Stop it. You're not that old."

"Older than you."

Adam stopped walking and pulled her to a halt. "Is that a problem as you see it?"

"No. No, it's not," she reassured him as she tugged him into motion again. "Really," she added when he looked at her a bit incredulously.

"Okay, that's good, because it's not an issue for me. At all." He ran his arm around her shoulders and pulled her close to his side. She snuggled in for warmth. It wasn't chilly, per se, but without the sun the breeze was cool.

They walked for a while longer then turned back to return to the complex. After taking turns rinsing off the sand at the rinse station by the short steps up from the beach, they slipped their flip-flops on and returned to their lanai.

"Do you want to have some coffee or another drink and sit outside for a while?" Adam asked.

"Coffee sounds nice. I can't get over how gorgeous it is. I'd hate to miss a moment by going to bed earlier than we have to."

"Oh, I don't know... I'm kind of looking forward to bedtime myself."

Tori's jaw dropped at his low, suggestive tone. And with that, Adam chuckled and went inside to make their coffee.

Come to think of it, I'm looking forward to it, too, she thought with a smile.

Chapter Ten

To simplify things and make the most of their space, Adam had volunteered to use the kids' bathroom, so he'd headed in with his stuff to get ready for bed while Tori was in the master bath. He wondered as he brushed his teeth when was the last time he'd been a bit nervous about sleeping with a woman...and by that he meant actually sleeping. To be honest, he hadn't ever really given it much thought before.

He'd tossed off that flirtatious remark earlier, but had immediately given himself a mental head-smack. Why had he even gone there when he was trying not to become more intimate?

Because he really, *really* wanted to. That was why.

He set his toothbrush aside and splashed some water on his face. If he didn't pull himself together and start being consistent, he was going to look like a complete idiot, or at the very least indecisive.

And speaking of indecisive—sleep pants or boxer briefs? He usually slept in the buff but...

Oh hell, might as well wear both. Probably be good as a reminder for his control.

He slipped on the items then walked back through to the living area. The door to the master was wide open.

"Tori?"

"Come on in." She padded barefoot out of the bathroom in a faded blue Cal Bears T-shirt that hung almost to her knees. It had the look of something that she wore a lot...and by its size and how boxy it was, it was obviously a man's shirt. After an initial smile at him, she was no longer looking at him, busy sorting through some clothes she'd unpacked into the dresser.

A twinge hit him in the gut. Whose shirt had she kept? It took him a moment to realise that he was jealous of some mystery man from her past. It was a pretty alien feeling and didn't sit well with him at all.

Turning away, he went to the window to look out on the subtly lit pool area and beyond to the palm trees silhouetted against the ocean. It was mostly quiet and the sound of the waves was soothing. "Is it okay with you if we leave the window open tonight?" he quietly asked over his shoulder.

"That sounds perfect." Her voice was closer than he'd anticipated. She slid her hands around his abdomen and laid her cheek against his bare back.

The conflicting emotions warring within were a new experience for him. He loved being close to her, but not knowing where he stood, not knowing what the future held when so much was at stake, left an uneasy edge to his joy in being with her.

He swallowed down his discontent and reached back to pull her around the front of him, wrapping his arms around her as they both looked out of the window together. He heard her yawn and had to smile.

"It's been a long, full day. Why don't we go to bed?" he prompted.

"Mmm, that's probably a good idea, but part of me doesn't want to miss a moment."

Adam knew what she meant. He turned and guided her away from the window and towards the bed. "You'll still be in Hawaii and listening to the waves all night while you get some sleep. What side would you like?"

She answered by crawling up on the bed and across to the side away from the window closest to the bathroom. The back of the tee rode up her legs and gave him a glimpse of something satiny and aqua. *More new lingerie?* He groaned.

Tori lifted the covers and slid between the sheets, lying on her side facing Adam. He knew as soon as her head hit the pillow that he wouldn't have much problem keeping it casual tonight. Her eyelids were already drooping.

He smiled at the sight she made, barely a bump in the covers of the big bed. He climbed in on his side and faced her, reaching out a hand to brush back a curl that had fallen across her temple near her eye.

"You didn't look very happy when you came into the room," she mumbled, though her sleepy gaze was direct.

Damn, she was observant. He decided to just put it out there. "I was just wondering whose shirt that was."

A line appeared between her eyebrows as she frowned. "What? This shirt? It's mine."

"I mean before... Who you got it from."

"Always been mine. I bought it about... Well, a long time ago. In college. Why? Did you think it was some ex-boyfriend's?"

He was sure his guilty expression gave him away.

"I'd like to think I'm not that crass," she chided gently. "Even if I *had* kept something like that, I wouldn't wear it to bed with my new..." She trailed off.

Adam wondered why she'd stopped. "Boyfriend?" he finished for her.

She looked away over his head towards the window. "Well, yes, I suppose."

Ouch. She supposes? Adam opened his mouth, a bit disconcerted that she was so reluctant to name him as such when they'd been dating for over a month. "You—"

She snapped her gaze back to meet his. "No! I'm sorry. That sounded bad. I just mean, a boyfriend sounds like something a teenager would have. I was trying to think of a more...adult term."

Relieved, Adam relaxed back onto the pillow. "Lover?" he suggested.

"Well..."

"No, I guess that wouldn't exactly fit yet either. Date?"

"We're more than just dates by now. I mean, who goes on a date to Hawaii?"

"Hmm..." Adam loved how serious her expression was as she tried to think, but at the same time she looked so sleepy. "Partners wouldn't work either. I think you'd have to be living together for that one to apply."

"Hmm..." she echoed as her eyes drifted closed then opened again. "How about...?"

He waited for her to finish her sentence, but her eyes blinked closed again and remained shut this time.

"I think that lovers and partners is the way we're headed, Tor," he whispered. "At least I hope so. That's why we're taking the scenic route."

Tori exhaled on a sigh and it looked as though a faint smile crossed her lips as she sank deeper into sleep.

* * * *

Tori found a safe place to stand and came up above the surface when Adam tapped her on the shoulder. He removed his snorkel from his mouth and said, "I think you're ready for some shade. You look pretty pink." Adam pressed a finger to her cheek then nodded as though to confirm his suspicions. "Yep. Definitely pink. Break time."

She followed suit and grimaced at the rubbery taste she was aware of now that she wasn't distracted by the wonders of the coral beds just offshore from their condo complex. "But I can see some really yellow fish I wanted to—"

"Later. Trust me. The fish will still be there, and we have a few days yet. Besides, I have a surprise for you."

"Another one?" He'd already surprised her this morning with a gift of what he'd called a rashguard, but was basically just a long-sleeved, swimsuit material shirt—to keep her from getting burned while they went snorkelling, he'd told her—then had shown her the snorkelling gear he'd gone to pick up before she'd woken up.

She glanced longingly one last time at the coral under the water then carefully followed Adam back ashore to the sand. There were actually trees growing along the edge of the grass and beach, so at this time of day, there were shady patches of sand. A few people had brought chairs down, some in the sun and some in the shade, but still there were barely a dozen people within sight in any direction. Adam had chosen their accommodations well.

After a quick rinse, they walked to their lanai. "Would you like a water?" Tori offered. But before she could open the screen door to go inside, Adam stopped her with a hand on her arm.

"Sure, but after that, why don't you take a shower and get cleaned up? We're going to take a short drive and then have dinner out. If that's okay?" he hastened to add.

Tori nodded, already beginning to understand just how much pleasure Adam took in planning and doing. It was actually really nice being on the receiving end of his enthusiasm for different activities, and she was happy to go along with his ideas. He hadn't hit a clunker yet...other than possibly the rock wall at the gym a couple of weeks ago. She'd got stuck frozen in place partway up the wall and couldn't force herself to go up or down, or let go. Adam had had to climb up to her and basically prise her fingers from the hand-holds to allow the belayer to lower her back to the floor.

So, if it didn't involve heights, she was open for anything he came up with.

"That sounds great. Should I wear anything specific?"

"How about the tropical print sundress I saw hanging in the closet? Oh, and bring a sweater."

"We're going to a luau, aren't we?" Tori chuckled at the crestfallen look on Adam's face at her having guessed his surprise. She crossed to him and gave him a light kiss. "I love that idea, and thank you for planning it. I think I would've figured it out when we pulled up at the venue anyway."

"That's true." When she would've backed away, he held her in place for one more lingering kiss. "Having fun?"

"The best fun of my life," she replied in a subconscious echo of her goals. Adam's expression sobered a bit and he released her from his embrace. She studied him. Not for the first time, she wondered if he indeed knew something about the *other* goal, the one she hadn't shared with him and never would. It was possible, since she had thought she'd noticed her notebooks being out of place the day he'd used her computer to check his email. At the time, she'd thought he might have just knocked them askew accidentally then put them back. She wouldn't have taken him for a snoop. But then again, human nature being what it was, curiosity might have got the better of him…

However, if he did know about that goal, why on earth hadn't they had sex yet?

Still puzzling over that, knowing that the answer wouldn't be forthcoming any time soon, she excused herself to get ready.

When she got into the bathroom and had stripped, she gave herself a once-over and grimaced when she saw the back of her neck. There was a definite line in the small area between the mock turtleneck of the rashguard and her hairline. She made a mental note to thank Adam both for the gift of the cover-up and for calling a halt to their snorkelling when he had. She had a reddish hue to her hair and was fair-skinned, but fortunately didn't burn as easily as her mother. Still, they were in the tropics, so it wasn't a matter of *if* she burned but rather to what degree. She'd need to make sure to slap sunscreen on more often tomorrow.

Tori got in the shower and washed her body and hair then added conditioner. While she left it in, she ran her hands back down her body and thought about the night to come. Last night had been all about sleeping, but she hoped to do more than sleep in that comfy bed tonight.

She smiled to herself and slid her slick hands back up to cup her breasts, gliding her thumbs over her nipples as she imagined Adam naked and wet on the other side of the wall. The thought sent a shot of lust through her and she gave them a tweak then soothed them with her palms. She felt the unmistakeable tingling in her pussy.

How many times had she masturbated since she'd met Adam? If the old wives' tale was true, she'd be blind by now.

She ran her hand down between her thighs and sent her fingers skating over her clit. Dipping a finger inside, she confirmed the slick feel of her juices and used them to lubricate her nub in earnest. By now she knew that, while shower gel worked well, nothing felt as good as the real thing.

After watching Adam's gorgeous body well on display all day in his suit, it didn't take her long to approach her climax. The final straw was imagining that Adam needed some toiletry item and knocked, but she couldn't hear over the water. So he walked in and watched her pleasuring herself, stroking his cock as he urged her on...

Oh God...

She threw a hand out against the wall and shuddered as she came hard, panting as though she'd just finished one of Adam's gruelling workouts. While she recovered, she mentally sorted through what she would wear to bed under her T-shirt tonight. Maybe nothing?

Brilliant. Nothing it is.

That reminded her of their conversation right before she'd fallen asleep. She couldn't believe he'd been jealous at the idea of her wearing another man's T-shirt to bed. Maybe she should ask him for one of his. Especially if it carried his scent. She loved the pure, masculine smell of him. He was intoxicating, even after working out, and whatever products he used for grooming weren't overpowering like a lot of men's.

Mmm…

For a moment she was tempted to bring herself off again, but the water had begun to cool and she reluctantly set aside her explorations and finished rinsing her hair.

Tori shut off the water and listened, noting that the other shower was still running. She wondered if Adam was doing some self-love of his own. The thought made her smile.

I will get what I want from you soon, Adam. But now… I think I want all the 'strings' in the world.

Would he want something serious at his age, though? Especially with someone hers?

Only time would tell. And speaking of time, it was time to get ready for what promised to be another wonderful evening with Adam.

Chapter Eleven

"That was wonderful," Tori enthused on the drive back to their condo. "I really got the feeling that the dancers were expressing their heritage and love of dance rather than just doing a job. Maybe that's an intentional part of what they do to be successful," she admitted, "but it was still amazing to watch."

Adam glanced away from the road to smile at Tori as she continued to recount the things she'd enjoyed about the luau and the dancing. Her love for life was really infectious and, as hard as he tried, he could never understand why she'd hidden herself in her work for so long. Everything they did seemed new to her, but she embraced it all with verve.

Well, he was selfishly glad that he was able to be with her through so many firsts. He found himself thinking daily about what else he could introduce her to. Of course, opening that line of thought often led to ideas that were less innocent fun but he knew would be just as entertaining.

Which in turn led to a lot of solo sessions in the shower.

Adam shifted in his seat as they pulled into the parking lot and he made his way to the spot in front of their door. "Home sweet home," he announced as he parked the rental car then turned off the engine.

The sudden quiet embraced them and when Tori didn't immediately open her door, he looked over to find her watching him.

"You are an incredible man, Adam Cross."

"You're the incredible one, Ms Warren. Wait there," he cautioned and opened his door. He got out and walked quickly around the car to open hers for her. She placed her hand in his and rose from her seat. He admired the flash of bare thigh when her wrap skirt parted as she stood then shrugged with a grin as she gave him a raised eyebrow.

"Hey, you can't blame a guy for looking." He closed and locked the car, then moved to open the condo.

"True. And guys aren't the only ones who look, you know."

As he held the door open, he turned to look at her enquiringly and caught her lifting her gaze from the direction of his ass. Then she waggled her eyebrows and winked.

He laughed loudly then quietened when she shushed him as she walked past him into their place. "People might be sleeping."

"Hmm, maybe. You shouldn't be so funny then. I can't help it if you make me laugh."

Adam went to start the Kona coffee brewing for their nightly cup on the lanai, then they each took a few minutes to freshen up and get comfortable. When he saw her emerge from the bedroom and walk out onto the lanai, Adam mourned the loss of the flattering dress with its tendency to billow open and show her legs. But, he thought as he fixed their mugs, he had to admit Tori was still sexy in anything she wore, even sweats and a T-shirt. Might even be sexier since she was tousled and scrubbed clean and looked ready to get cosy with for the night.

And who knew what she had on under the casual wear? She had a seemingly endless supply of lingerie and he always anticipated what she would wear next. Of course, the fact that it seemed to be a concerted effort at seduction took a bit of the lustre from it, but he'd be lying to himself if he didn't admit it was working.

He brought the coffees with him outside, handed Tori hers then sat down on the lounger next to hers.

"So what do you have lined up for tomorrow?"

He gave her what he hoped was an innocent look, though he'd already known he'd have to reveal the plans tonight so they could prepare. "What makes you think I have something planned?"

"I know you by now, and I'm pretty sure you have every day of this trip thought out."

"How did you like the snorkelling today?" he veered off in a seeming change of topic, though her answer had everything to do with what he had lined up for the next day.

Her eyes lit up. "Loved it," she answered quickly and succinctly, her expression one of anticipation. He debated teasing her by making her wait until bedtime to find out, or maybe telling her they were going shopping or something, but in the end that begging gaze got to him.

"How about a snorkelling trip, first out to Molokai crater and then to see sea turtles?" he revealed.

"Oh my God, that would be so much fun!" She slammed down her mug with a wobble and launched herself onto his lap, peppering him with kisses.

He chuckled as he closed his arms around her and settled her more comfortably against him. "You don't get seasick, do you?" he checked, though he had some Sea-Bands and Dramamine with him just in case.

"I have no idea," she said happily. "And I don't care if I do. I can suck it up for a day."

Hopefully those wouldn't prove to be famous last words.

"We have to get up early," he cautioned. "Though that shouldn't be too hard with the time change working in our favour. They said to be there, ready to go, at six. It's just over at the harbour, so less than ten minutes' drive."

"Oh that's convenient. So we just, what, wear our suits? Do we have to bring our own snorkelling gear? Oh, and what about food?"

He lightly ran his hand over her bare forearm, feeling her skin goosebump after his touch. "They serve a light breakfast onboard during the trip out, and lunch on the way back, and they provide the masks, snorkels and fins. So really, we just need to wear our suits and cover-ups and pack a bag with sunscreen, hats, towels, water bottles—that sort of thing."

"Nice." She sighed and snuggled in against his chest. "See? You would've had to have told me soon anyway, especially when you set the alarm."

Adam closed his eyes, enjoying the feel of her cradled against him. "True."

They lay together for a few minutes longer, listening to the waves. Finally, Tori stirred. "I think we should get you into bed, mister. You're falling asleep."

He really wasn't the least bit sleepy, actually, but bed with Tori sounded good.

She made to get up, but he tightened his hold on her then swung his legs to the side and stood with her still in his arms.

"What about the mugs?" she asked. "Here, I can get them—bend down a little."

He moved as she instructed and she grabbed first her cup then his. He managed to get the screen door sliding open with his foot, then left it open. He'd come back and close up in a minute.

Tori grinned as he carried her all the way into the kitchen, then let her slowly slide down his body until she was on her feet. He took the cups from her over her protests to rinse them and place them in the dishwasher.

"Okay, I'll get the back door then." She walked back into the living area then closed and locked the door.

Adam emptied out his backpack onto the bed in the kids' room to begin sorting what they'd need for the next day. They got everything packed and ready, then started to get ready for bed. He was already in his side of the bed when Tori walked out of the master bathroom, once again clad in her Cal Bears T-shirt.

Unlike the night before, tonight she looked wide awake when she crawled in on her side. He held his arms open in invitation and she immediately came to press herself against him.

"I thought you were tired," she murmured against his neck.

"Nope. You?"

"Nope," she repeated and kissed his throat. She slid her smooth leg against his until she had manoeuvred it between his, aligning them even more closely.

His cock, which had been semi-hard most of the evening in spite of his shower jack-off session before the luau, began to fill even more. With her pressed against him, he had no way of disguising his arousal, especially with just two thin layers of cotton over it.

He ran his hand down to her lower back and pressed her lower body more tightly against him. He had purposely not brought protection so he wouldn't be tempted to throw his plans to the wind, but he knew they wouldn't be going to sleep tonight without both of them coming—not if he had anything to say about it.

"Mmm… You feel great." She lifted her head and he lowered his to kiss her deeply. It was heaven stroking his tongue into her mouth, teasing and tangling with hers as she undulated against him.

The kiss began to escalate in heat and she ran her hand down his back and under the waistbands of his briefs and pyjamas to cup his ass.

"Oh God," he gasped, surging against her as she teased her fingers along the sensitive crease between buttock and thigh. He slanted across her mouth in a torrid mating of lips and tongues as he slid his palm over her ass until he reached her warm thigh.

He then ran his hand back up under the T-shirt…and found nothing impeding his progress over her ass, all the way to her lower back.

"Naughty girl. Did you run out of lingerie?"

"Oh no. I just chose to go without tonight. You like?"

"Hell yes." He gave a pull that landed her on top of him, their legs scissored. She moved to straddle his hips, with her uncovered pussy riding along the ridge of his erection. He yanked her down on top of him so that her unfettered breasts moulded against his chest. He could feel the points of her nipples even through the barrier of her top. She took charge of the kiss this time, darting her tongue into his mouth and nipping lightly at his lower lip.

Now that he had both hands free, he cupped her ass and rhythmically kneaded and urged her into motion against him. The friction was intense and he thrust up against her. Suddenly, she sat up, grasped her shirt and pulled it up over her head, baring herself entirely to his view for the first time.

"You're beautiful, Tori." He loved her colouring, from the pale pink nipples that matched her lips, to her creamy complexion and her neatly trimmed pussy that proved beyond a shadow of a doubt that she was a natural redhead. He released her ass to slide his hands up her back, urging her chest downwards to his waiting mouth.

He lifted his head to draw one perfect peak into his mouth, rolling it between his tongue and teeth and teasing it until it was swollen and reddened and she was moaning. He lay back, admiring his handiwork, then took her hint as she offered the other one to him. He applied himself to the other side and spanned his hand over her hip, letting it ride there as she rocked against him.

Adam had to taste her. In a quick move, he flipped them so that she was on her back with hardly a break in his attentions to her breast. Moving upwards, he licked and sucked his way up her neck to her ear then placed a firm kiss on her lips before sitting back on his heels.

He took a moment to enjoy the view of her breathless and naked beneath him and gave her a smile, which she returned. The smile slowly melded into a gaze of anticipation as Adam began to scoot down the bed until he was flat on his belly between her thighs.

"Adam…" She began to raise herself up and he placed a gentle hand on her belly.

"Shh, just lay back and enjoy."

He kissed first the inside of one thigh, then the other. Blowing gently on her pussy got a hip-tossing response, so before he began he grasped her hips in his hands and held her firmly to the mattress.

"Oh God, oh God…" Tori moaned, arching against his restraint.

He nibbled over from her thigh along the soft skin there then worked his tongue through her folds to part them. His first taste of her was ambrosia, salt and tart on his tongue, and he delved for more before sliding his mouth up to encompass her clit and suck.

"Ah! Oh, holy crap…" Tori reached down to grab his hair, but far from trying to pull him away, she was pressing him even closer. He released one hip to use that hand to tease at her nub while thrusting his tongue into her core, then reversing the action.

He worked with his lips and tongue and fingers until Tori gave his hair a yank then scrabbled to get a grip on his shoulders in a way that sent a clear message. If her actions hadn't made it clear, she groaned, "Fuck me, oh God, Adam, do it."

Fuck. "No protection, hon."

"Oh God, are you fucking kidding — mmph — "

Adam had moved quickly up her while she was talking and silenced her with a kiss while he continued to fuck her with his fingers, working her clit with his thumb. It didn't take more than a minute before she was arching and thrusting up against him, moaning into his mouth as she came, her pussy rhythmically pulsating against his fingers.

He eased her down from her climax with increasingly gentle kisses, though he was feeling frantic himself. He palmed his aching erection through his pyjamas.

"Jesus, Adam, if you don't at least finish in front of me, I'm going to think... Well, I don't know what I'll think, but I want to see you come. Come on," she encouraged. "Come on me."

Fuck it. He knelt up and shoved his pants down, raking his hard cock in the process, though he was so far gone the discomfort didn't faze him in the least. He moved the hand he'd been fingering her with to delve once more into her wet pussy then used that to lubricate his erection.

Watching her rapt face as she gazed alternately between his eyes and his hand on his cock was all he needed. With less than a dozen strokes, he was coming, jetting cum onto her bare abdomen, filling her belly button and streaking her with his release.

She reached down to rub it onto her skin and he shuddered one more time, panting.

"Looks like I'll need another shower," she teased huskily.

He ran his hand over his sweat-slickened chest, enjoying how hungrily she watched its progress, then grinned. "I think I do, too." He leant down and added in a whisper, "But not nearly as long as my usual ones."

Chapter Twelve

It was almost brutal going back to reality after their trip, and it wasn't like Tori even had to go back to work. She couldn't imagine having to go back to her usual job after such a mellow and relaxing trip.

They had turned in the rental car and gone through security, and were sitting in the terminal waiting for their flight when Tori's phone rang. She was startled—no one had called her cellphone the whole trip except for Adam once when he'd been at the ABC Store to ask whether she'd like dark or milk chocolate when he'd seen a good deal on chocolate-covered macadamia nuts. She hoped nothing was wrong with her parents.

After scrambling a bit to get it from her purse, she answered hurriedly, "Hello?"

"Victoria? Are you avoiding me?"

At the sound of the familiar but not exactly welcome voice she sat back and checked the display to confirm that, yes, it was Terrence. "No, I'm not avoiding you. I'm on vacation."

"I know, but come on... This is an important lunch and I figured the funding was worth a few hours of your time—"

"Wait, what? I have no idea what you're talking about." Tori frowned, trying to hear Terrence over the gate attendant as she made an announcement.

"I put it all in the emails."

"What emails? Look, Terrence, when I said I was on vacation, I didn't just mean my sabbatical. I meant I'm in Hawaii at the moment." Out of the corner of her eye, she saw Adam turn his head towards her. She looked at him and shrugged.

Terrence moaned dramatically. "Oh no. Freaking Hawaii? Jesus, Victoria, could you have picked a worse time to spread your wings?"

She closed her eyes, striving for patience. "Look, pretend I have no clue what you mean, since that's exactly what the case is, and tell me from the beginning why you're calling me, what was in the emails and what lunch?"

Terrence sighed and paused for a moment. "Okay, so I emailed you a few days ago because a few key people in our division have been invited by the powers that be to attend a work lunch. I mean, these people are all the way up in the adminisphere, the ones who control the budget for our line. You were on the shortlist to attend, but of course you're off work. Still, we could really use you there to talk up our line and, well... It would be a good thing. So I was asked to see if you'd come even though you're on sabbatical. And now you're in Hawaii and rumour has it that there are cuts coming and we don't want to be on the chopping block."

Tori frowned, suddenly worried about the funding for her experiments being cut. "When is the lunch?"

"Tomorrow."

"Tomorrow..." Tori pulled her phone away from her ear to check the time then looked at her boarding pass. Doing some quick mental math, she said cautiously, "I don't want you to get excited, but I might be able to make it. I'm actually flying home tonight. What time?"

"I would love you forever if you could make it." Terrence sounded pathetically relieved. "There's no one who can speak about our progress and goals like you can. It's at the banquet room at Tini's Bistro at Cambridge Crossing at twelve-thirty. I can pick you up at noon?"

"I'll just meet you there. No need for you to get me," she protested.

"Are you sure? I think I should —"

"You just don't want me to change my mind. Don't worry, I'll be there. Besides, I probably won't be coming from home, but the gym." She was set to resume her regular schedule with Adam tomorrow. She smiled his way, but he was busy studying his boarding pass.

"I really want to update you on what's been going on so that you're prepared," Terrence persisted. "I'll pick you up at your gym then. Del Sol, that really big, expensive one, right? At noon."

Tori bit back a sigh since she knew from experience there was no sense in arguing once he'd decided on a course of action. His stubbornness was one of the reasons they'd not worked well as a couple, though his persistence came in handy at work.

"Fine — meet me at the gym at noon, and we can talk on the way to the restaurant." The gate attendant was making another garbled announcement and some people around them started standing up. "I really have to go. I'll see you tomorrow."

"Okay, Victoria. Thank you so much. I really appreciate it."

They said their goodbyes and Tori hung up her phone and turned to Adam. "Was that our boarding call?"

He gave her a quick sideways glance and shook his head.

"It was something about our flight, though, right?"

"Pre-boarding. Anxious to get home?" Adam's question had an edge to it and she turned to fully face him.

"In a way, yes," she answered slowly, trying to figure out what was behind his abrupt change in mood. Had it been Terrence's call? "I mean, all else being equal, I'd rather be back at the beach and not have to leave Hawaii, but I also don't want to sit around in the airport all day."

"And you have an important lunch date to get back for tomorrow. If that guy's picking you up tomorrow at noon, you know we're going to have to cut back some things we usually do, like spending my lunch together after our workout."

Oh. "That's true. I'm sorry about making other plans without talking to you first, but Terrence was practically begging and—"

"That's okay," Adam interrupted. "It's not like we had anything formal planned. Just a habit. And you couldn't turn down someone begging you for your time." He shrugged, obviously trying to pull off nonchalance, but Tori could tell that he was upset.

She tucked her hand through the crook of his elbow where it lay on the armrest between their seats. "What's wrong? Is it that I've scheduled something during the time we usually spend together? Or," she added with a growing sense of what the problem was, "is it because I'm being picked up by Terrence and having lunch with him?"

He didn't answer right away, so she continued, "Because if that's what's got you in this mood, you need to understand that this is purely a work thing." She explained about the lunch and the connection to her funding. "And Terrence is one of the other research scientists in the loop on what I had to put on hold, so he needs to update me on what's been happening since I left work."

"So you guys are just co-workers? Because the way you talked to him sounded like you have some kind of history or something."

Tori gaped at him for a second. "You're really jealous." She couldn't believe it.

"I'm not jealous, I just...want to know where we stand."

The call for boarding for their section came then and Tori let that slide for the moment while they gathered their belongings then boarded the plane. She knew that she would have a captive audience for the five-plus hours they'd be on the flight.

They settled in their seats on the right side of the big, double-aisled plane. After take-off, Tori resumed their conversation.

"Okay, you say you're not jealous, that you want to know where you stand... I assume you mean with me, as a couple. I'm not sure what you want me to say. I mean, what exactly isn't clear?"

Adam shrugged.

"Oh no. We're not doing the not talking thing. What is it?"

"Just forget I said anything." Adam finally looked at her and his expression softened. "I'm just being stupid. Let's not end the great time we had on the trip on this note."

"Adam, I just want to understand what you meant by that. Obviously, at the time you said it, you had something specific in mind that you aren't certain of with us." She looked away at the back of the seat in front of hers. "Maybe I'm just being stupid now, but I just can't figure out what changed."

"You're not stupid. You're the smartest person I know, way smarter than I am. And I get that it's about work. It's all good."

Tori sighed, frustrated. "It's not all good. What the hell? Now you're putting yourself down?"

Adam swallowed and his jaw clenched. "Look. Tori, you are smart. And so is this Terrence guy. You both have doctorates and do important research. I honestly just don't understand what you find interesting about me or that we really have in common. You'd...be better off with someone like him."

Her jaw dropped. *What the...?* "You are so motivational and dedicated. You enjoy life and treat me like a queen. We're attracted to each other and we've never had a problem talking to each other about anything, at least until today. Why would you think that I'd be better off with a pretentious jackass like Terrence?"

That earned her a faint smile. "Pretentious jackass, huh?"

"Yes, I like you much better than Terrence. Okay? That's about as straightforward as I can be. We've always been on the same page up until now, so can this ridiculous, bizarre conversation be over, please? I want to finish this trip with the Adam I started it with." She tried with her eyes to communicate her desire to reassure him of his place in her life.

Adam picked up her hand and kissed the back of it. "Nothing more about all of that. You're right. I suppose there are always going to be arguments and misunderstandings, but as long as we're honest and forthcoming about things, I doubt we'll have many bizarre conversations." He didn't relinquish her hand and she sat back to simply enjoy being near him.

And if a part of her brain whispered that she wasn't exactly being forthcoming to Adam with her summer goals, it was easy enough to shove that aside, knowing that she thought of him as being much more than she had in the beginning. And those goals had nearly been met, and when they were complete, she could mentally move on.

Chapter Thirteen

Irritated, Tori blew a piece of hair out of her peripheral vision with more violence than it warranted. The past two months had been an exercise in extreme frustration, so she hit the bag in front of her with extreme prejudice.

Oh, not everything was bad. In fact, two of her three sabbatical goals were going swimmingly. Complete successes. Her workouts with Adam were really starting to pay dividends, and he had introduced her to all sorts of new activities she wouldn't have previously considered, which combined exercise and fun. They'd been hiking, biking, rollerblading and canoeing. She'd been hooked up to a harness and gone rock climbing. Swimming was now part of her regular routine, and they'd played tennis several times.

Adam wasn't all about fitness, either. There had been the mind-blowingly romantic trip to Hawaii. They'd also done several day trips around home. One weekday Adam had been free, they'd devoted the whole day to browsing through a museum—and, ironically, *that* was the day that had been the toughest on her feet. In response, that night he'd given her a foot massage and pedicure, painting her toenails a beautiful coral pink they'd impulsively picked out together at an all-night drugstore. Ever since that first time she'd shown up at his place with her toenails done, to his admiration, she'd made sure to keep them done and having him suggest trying to do it himself had turned out to be a lot of fun, and sexy to boot.

They'd been on a ton of 'normal' dates as well— movies and dinners, and a summer concert in the park.

And they still hadn't got past third base.

Tori punched the bag again, feeling violent.

It was enough to make a girl want to buy a battery-operated best friend.

Punch.

All that physical exertion.

Punch, punch.

All the romantic dates.

Punch, kick.

It was as if Adam had decided to become the perfect boyfriend and spoil her for all others. Except he hadn't consulted her, but had relied on his grandma's advice about saving it for the marriage bed.

Kick, punch, punch, kick.

And her sabbatical was over. It was Labor Day, and she was going back to work tomorrow. *Damn it.* And no sex in sight.

"Whatever you're thinking about, you're really pummelling the bag, sweetheart," Adam praised from where he was keeping the bag from swinging for her. "Great job."

"Thanks," Tori muttered, still focused on the end of her summer. Only one more night, then it was over. Suddenly, an idea hit her.

One more night...

She back away from the bag, indicating she was done. "Are you free later?"

Adam's eyebrows shot up as he handed her a towel then pulled together into a frown. "Of course. Aren't we going to the blues festival together?"

Tori flushed, which she hid by mopping her face. Sometimes, she let her mouth get ahead of her brain, and it happened more often than she liked around Adam. It was a wonder he thought she was intelligent at all—she could be such a ditz and he was always so collected and together.

"I meant afterwards. Do you want to come over? I thought maybe we could celebrate the end of my sabbatical together."

For some reason, Adam's mouth twitched, as if he was trying not to smile, maybe? Suspicious, she watched him with narrowed eyes, but he was instantly back to his usual calm self.

"I'd love to. You have a lot to celebrate. You've done a fantastic job of successfully meeting your personal goals for your time off, and I've been honoured to be a part of it."

Ha! If he only knew...

"Say, why don't you pack a bag?" Tori suggested in an oh-by-the-way tone of voice, striving to sound offhand and casual about it. "After being out at the festival, you'll probably want to clean up before we, uh, celebrate. You can plan on showering at my place." *Oh, real smooth there, Ms Worldly Wise. Might as well just say flat out—you're spending the night, big boy, so come prepared for a slumber party.*

Was that another twitch? No, just rubbing his lips together.

"Great idea, thanks for thinking of my comfort. In fact, I'll bring a few different outfits in case our plans take an unexpected turn." Adam turned his brilliant smile on her, and she could almost feel her brain cells melting. What exactly did he mean by that? Tori shook her head. All she knew for sure was she would have him right where she wanted him – in her bed, one way or another – before this sabbatical was officially over.

Or she'd die trying.

Adam was going to die trying...not to laugh.

Not *at* Tori. That would be mean, and he knew by now that he was falling in love with her – if he wasn't already there – crazy ideas and all. But the whole situation was getting farcical. She wanted him. He wanted her. *She* was going to pull out all the stops to have sex tonight so she'd meet her goal. *He* was going to do everything in his power to *not* have sex with her until after her sabbatical was over in order to prove a point. Adam rolled his eyes. What a screwball comedy this was turning out to be.

But the end was in sight, either way. Tori's time off had come to a close and one way or another they were soon going to finally make love.

Adam ignored the twinge of arousal that hit him and waved goodbye as they left the arena to head to their respective locker rooms. He would pack a bag for tonight. He would even let her manoeuvre him into having him spend the night – and he couldn't wait to see what reason she'd come up with for that. As for the sex, he figured if he could just hold out until morning, the sabbatical would be over, and their coming together would be less about fulfilling an objective, and more about expressing their connection and love.

Somehow, tonight had taken on talismanic properties in Adam's mind. If he gave in before the night was over, it would doom their incipient relationship to failure. But if he could just hold out till morning — *and not a moment longer,* his cock joined the conversation uninvited — he would have a chance at winning her, for good. Forever.

And the hardest two months of his life would have been worth it.

The hardest...and the best. With sex out of the picture, Adam had been forced to get close to her in other ways, and he had been surprised to find he enjoyed all the time they spent together — the long conversations, trying new activities together, making the most of the summertime. He'd fallen in love with her without even trying. But oh, by the end of those days...

He groaned as the memories assailed him. All the cold showers. All the solo sessions at home after their dates — and occasionally in the car when he knew he couldn't make it home. Oh, and a couple of times in her bathroom. Luckily for him, she seemed to lose track of time when she was doing dishes.

He'd had to set himself a strict no-penetration rule, or else he would never have been able to pull it off. And Tori, as sexy as she was, just wasn't quite brazen enough to force the issue on her own. Adam had gambled on her innate reserve keeping her from doing something irrevocable, like pulling his cock out and climbing on. That would've been game over in a heartbeat.

As that thought occurred to him, Adam began to get nervous about what she had in store for tonight.

He'd throw a towel in the car. Maybe he'd have time to yank off between the festival and her house. Some timely self-love? Might be the only difference between success and failure.

He was competitive, but this was about more than winning. Because part of losing at this game, Adam was afraid, would be losing his heart in the process.

And that was the one thing he couldn't risk.

* * * *

"That was great. I'd never even really listened to blues before, but it's definitely perfect to hear and see live."

Adam smiled in mellow agreement and used the arm that was around her shoulders to give her a squeeze as they strolled back to his car. He'd been oddly insistent about driving separately and meeting her there—something about running late—but for some reason, Tori'd sensed an off note to the seemingly innocent request. So she'd insisted in turn that he come pick her up, even if it would make them late for the headliner. Carpooling was in, right?

Once that strange snafu had been dealt with, they'd had a fantastic time. Her shoulder notched under his felt just right—really, the whole relationship felt just right. She even forgot their age difference most of the time, and when it did come up, it really had ceased to be important. Adam was just Adam, not some random twenty-something anymore.

Arriving back at her place, Adam pulled an overnight bag out of the back seat and snatched up a hand towel that had been under it. *Hand towel?* At her quizzical look, he slowly went a dull red. "Just picking up," Adam mumbled, paradoxically stuffing the towel under the driver's seat. He then grabbed her carryall and the backpack cooler and headed towards the condo, leaving a bemused Tori with only the blanket to carry.

"Mind if I take that shower?" he asked once they'd unpacked their gear and she'd started doing the dishes they had taken along for their wine and snacks.

Tori smiled to herself. So far so good. "Go ahead. You can use the master suite. It has a better showerhead." At least she hoped, or else she was going to look pretty stupid saying that. She wasn't exactly a showerhead connoisseur—she hardly ever took showers, preferring baths. In fact, she'd probably taken more showers at the gym in the past couple of months than in the previous ten years combined.

No. Tori didn't really know what the showerhead quality was like. But her shower had one thing the guest shower didn't—a see-through glass door.

Chapter Fourteen

Oh, thank God, Adam thought as he closed the bathroom door and quickly stripped down. He winced as he eased the zipper of his shorts down over the heated flesh barely contained by his smallest jock. Taking care not to hook his stiff erection as he pulled his clothes the rest of the way off, he stepped into the shower, already scoping out her products for something nice and slippery.

Citrus shower gel? He tested it between his fingers. *Perfect.*

Adam wetted down hastily, and quickly shampooed his hair and rinsed. Then he squirted a dollop of shower gel into his hand, worked up a lather and haphazardly soaped up and rinsed off before squeezing another palmful out.

His poor neglected cock jumped as he took it in his slippery grip. "Ahh," he breathed aloud, before remembering he needed to be quiet. Mouth parted in an effort to get more air, he closed his eyes and pictured Tori as she'd been today, leaning back companionably against his chest while they'd watched the musicians from their blanket at the festival. The plunging V neckline of her woven cotton top had gaped, and with his bird's-eye view from above and behind her, he'd caught a glimpse more than once of a surprisingly delicate pink tip. No bra. Something — the friction of the shirt? — had her nipples puckered every single time his gaze was drawn to them. And it was drawn often. From his voyeuristic vantage point, he couldn't miss them, pressing outward against her lovingly clingy top, constantly hard.

Kinda like me.

The image was working, and as he approached his climax, he masochistically paused for one last squirt of shower gel.

That was when the shower door opened.

Adam jolted in surprise, his jaw dropping as he took in the vision of Tori sans clothing. She was stunning, with those ever-perked nipples mouth-wateringly bare, and creamy skin everywhere. Unable to stop his eagerly wandering eyes, he had to take a deep breath as he watched her approach the shower, confirmed that, yes, she *was* looking at him with a predatory look in her eyes. Predatory...and hotter than hell.

He'd seen the difference her workouts over the summer had made to her extremities and her endurance. For the first time, he was seeing her core and the total physical picture, and he felt a moment of deep pride for her that had the blessed effect of taking the edge off his arousal. Along with that, her self-confidence had grown and she wore it well.

"So are you coming out, or am I coming in? Because it's a shame to waste that" — she nodded at his unabated erection — "on my shower gel." Her voice was husky but certain, her face glowing with admiration, and Adam knew he was sunk.

Firming his jaw with determination and trying not to let his disappointment show through, he finally gave in to all he'd been struggling against for the past couple of months. He just couldn't fight it anymore. And if for some reason Tori stuck with her thought that this was a no-strings affair and this time was all he was going to get, Adam was going to make sure it was the best ever—for both of them.

He made quick work of rinsing and turning off the water. It was a struggle to keep from coming as he made sure all of the soap was off his cock.

Tori took a step backwards, tempting him from the shower with her body just out of reach. She smiled at him, but he couldn't return it right away and he watched as her brow puckered. Must be picking up his vibe. Adam cleared his head of everything except how damn sexy she looked standing there, assured as could be. Once he'd relaxed, he didn't have to fake the smile of appreciation he sent her way as he towelled off, unabashedly drying his balls and erection as she boldly watched.

Blindly tossing the towel over the shower door, he walked straight towards her, cock and hands making contact at the same time as he pulled her up flush against him. Her skin was so smooth and cool to the touch, it felt like sneaking a fingerful of whipped cream. Running his hands down her back to cup her full buttocks, he gave a heft and lifted a surprised but willing Tori off her feet. Without coaching, she instinctively wrapped her legs around Adam's waist, hooking her ankles behind him as he walked them into the bedroom and straight to the bed.

Adam loved how petite and perfect she felt in his arms, but didn't say anything—it didn't seem like the time to speak. So he kept his enjoyment to himself, instead showing her without words how utterly alluring he found her as he bent his head to learn the texture of her nipple with his tongue. His months of pent-up imaginings were finally being set free, without constraint. She was beautiful and responsive as she arched and moaned beneath him.

Tracing a hand down her trim abdomen then rounding the flare of her hip, he reached her silky thigh and traced back up her inner leg, unerringly finding the springy curls between her legs. A foray with his fingers found her slick and heated core, and it took every ounce of restraint not to bury himself inside her right then and there. Instead, he slipped downward, reluctantly leaving her breast and glancing up as he settled himself between her thighs.

Tori was in heaven. With her goal in sight, she couldn't have cared less about her original plan to seduce him in order to meet all three objectives. *God, I'm an idiot. A geeky idiot.* She would burn those damn notebooks.

"Oh God," she cried helplessly as Adam used his tongue to separate her folds while he spread her own juices up over her engorged clit. Like a bombshell, her climax hit without warning, faster than she would ever have thought possible.

"Yeah, babe. C'mon." Adam's encouraging moan against her clit was her first clue that he didn't intend to stop any time soon. Holy crap, she didn't know if she could take any more.

Alternately using his mouth and fingers, he tormented her while she shamelessly bared herself for his efforts, her new flexibility making her completely, erotically vulnerable to his attentions. As she soared over the precipice a second time, he licked and nibbled his way back up her body, paying torturous attention to her nipples as he used the glide of her juices to rub his erection right against her clit.

"Please!" she begged, and he slammed his mouth down on hers, sharing the taste of herself on his lips and tongue.

She threaded her fingers through his soft waves and held him to her as she deepened the kiss, inviting his plunder wantonly. Parting from her lips lingeringly, he raised his head to meet her gaze.

"I'll be right back."

Tori gaped until she figured out what he needed. "That drawer," she pointed, and blushed as Adam withdrew the brand new box of condoms she'd about died buying. Who knew there were so many freaking kinds? Thankfully, a female pharmacist had taken pity on her and walked her through her options. "Are those okay?" she asked anxiously before mentally smacking herself. *Oh, c'mon.*

Fortunately Adam overlooked her wimpy question, looking down from where he knelt over her. "Perfect. Just like you." He opened the box and extracted a packet, offering it to her and grinning as she shook her head frantically.

"You do it."

Adam laughed. "You have a doctorate, and you're scared to put on a condom." He opened the foil and placed the disc against the tip of his cock, then startled her by grabbing her hand. "Here. I'll hold the tip while you slick it down." He waited patiently as she tentatively touched the edges of the roll, fingertips feeling the silky, firm heat beneath.

Adam's breath caught. "C'mon, Tori." He formed her hand into a sheath. "Now roll it down, more pressure. Ah. Yeah, that's it."

With growing confidence, she finally smoothed the condom in place and gave Adam a few more strokes for good measure. A slow smile of pure womanly power crossed her face, and she forgot to be nervous as he poised at her entrance, waiting for her complete attention as he slowly filled her.

Oh. It had been years, but even then, it had never felt like this. Adam's girth stretched her in a deliciously carnal way, but it was his utter focus on her, the loving attention he paid—watching every nuance of her expression—that made her come to a sudden realisation.

She had never been made love to.

But Adam was making love to her right then. Her summer fling was in love with her.

And I'm in love with him.

Her breath shuddered from her, and she drove her hips up against him, needing to be closer, to affirm that he wasn't going anywhere. Her urgency was contagious, and they surged together, trying to make up for all the lost time at once, trying to make it last. Tori felt herself breaking apart. Wanting—needing—to watch Adam's face, she struggled to keep her eyes from closing with repletion. Her regard snared Adam's attention, and as if it was the final blow to his control, he began to chant her name, then froze, braced above her.

Rocking a few erratic times before lowering himself gently atop her, Adam seemed in no hurry to leave. He wrapped himself around her and they drifted down together from their completion. The new and overwhelming emotions in Tori had her clinging to him—her rock of the past three months—seeking contact in a newfound need for reassurance.

Finally—reluctantly, it seemed—Adam separated from her to briefly clean up. Tori was gratified by the eagerness Adam showed in returning to his place in her arms. She held him close as she tried to think of a way to break the silence and say the things that needed to be said.

His question came as a surprise. "Would you be mad if I told you I know about the other sabbatical goal?"

Oh God. Tori had to see his face. She pulled away just enough to make eye contact, but his carefully blank expression didn't give her much to go on. "That's not what this was all about," she protested, then closed her eyes as she amended, "Well, maybe at first, but not tonight. Oh, Adam, do you hate me?"

The mask on his face cracked, and a hopeful but wary expression emerged. "Of course I don't hate you, Tori." He paused, searching her eyes. "I love you," he added in a low tone, watching her closely.

Tori couldn't keep back the surge of joy at his softly spoken words. "Oh." She tackled him back against the bed. "I love you too." She began kissing him, and he laughed as he cooperated fully in her attack, before folding her close against his heart.

The chronically curious part of her had to ask. "So. When did you find out?"

He cleared his throat. "Two months ago."

"When you used the computer?"

He shifted enough to meet her eyes with a surprised expression. "Yes. How did you know?"

"You'd make a lousy spy. You put the notebooks back in the wrong order, you snoop."

Adam smiled ruefully. "Do you hate me?" he tossed her question of earlier back at her with a confident smile.

She couldn't even joke about it. "Of course I don't hate you, Adam. I love you." It was a playful echo of his response, but she seriously meant every word, and her heart soared as they met in a tender kiss.

"You did it, Tori. You made your sabbatical count."

"We did it," she corrected. "I couldn't have done any of it without you." She paused, adding impishly. "Oh, and I've put the notebooks with my *new* goals in them in a much better hiding place."

FALLING FOR
THE OTHER
BROTHER

Dedication

To my readers, thanks for all your support.

Chapter One

A cool waft of air on her shower-warm skin was the only warning Erica received before large hands cupped her bare shoulders. Once she got over her initial surprise, a smile curved her lips. The familiar touch meant that Trevor's last-minute flight home must have been on time. She was pulled back flush against a hard male body.

Or maybe she should say, a hardening male body.

She gave a little wiggle, bringing their bodies in closer alignment as her favourite rain-shower setting softly pelted them from above, with two slightly more forceful jets massaging from each side.

A muscular and extremely tanned arm reached past her to pluck the hand-held shower head from its holder.

"Picked up a little sun?" she joked. "I see you've been working hard."

Trevor's deep responding chuckle reverberated in her ear. "I always make time for play. In the Caribbean especially. And the shoot was on the beach."

As a popular and successful fitness model, Trevor did a lot of cover shoots and spreads for various magazines, as well as demonstrations for equipment. It was one of these demo jobs, evidently staged on a tropical beach, that he had just returned from.

"That must've been brutal." Erica gave a shudder, partly from the thought of the unrelenting sun and partly because, as she watched, Trevor was skimming his hand along her abdomen up to cup her breast. The contrast of her pale skin with his sun-darkened fingers was startling and extremely erotic, and the deliberately light, teasing touch sent a shiver through her.

She felt his shrug. He never complained about the less romantic aspects of his job, but was just happy to be doing what he did. No false modesty or dissembling, he enjoyed using his fit body to make a living.

"It was fine. Not as hot as you might think, just sunny."

Erica turned within his embrace and gave him a lingering welcome-back kiss. She was torn — glad to see him home early but dreading the conversation she had finally psyched herself up to initiate.

But not yet. Like Scarlett, she'd think about that tomorrow.

Firmly turning her mind from anything remotely cerebral, she instead lost herself in the hedonistic sensation of turning her pleasure over to the sexiest man she'd ever known. She knew the moment he sensed her acquiescence. The hands cruising over her slick back slid purposefully down to cup her buttocks. A satisfied hum in his throat was barely audible but somehow captured her focus.

Wanting to cause that sound again, she mirrored the movement of his hands. She could barely make a dent in his muscular ass, even when she gave a hard squeeze. Squeaking as he playfully returned the favour, the teasing evolved into a wet, sensuous game of follow-the-leader that soon had her panting with desire.

Erica was jarred from her reverie as Trevor abruptly ended the exploration and guided her to sit upon the ledge at the back of the walk-in shower. She jolted as her heated body touched the cool tile.

"Wha—"

"Shh. You'll see," Trevor cautioned, smirking as he adjusting the setting on the hand-held shower head from rain to a pulsing jet.

Oh my God. Erica moaned as he directed the spray across her sensitive peaks, twisting as he unrelentingly followed her movements with the almost torturous attention. She breathed a sigh of relief as he moved on, leaving her nipples aching in his wake, and continued upwards to her neck.

This time, her groan was one of utter bliss as she dropped her head forward to accommodate the impromptu massage. "Trev, that's perfect."

"Mmm," he agreed, using the stream to methodically tenderize her chronically tense shoulders into something resembling melty goo.

Just when she'd almost forgotten the sexual tension, he ratcheted it back up by trailing the jet swiftly down her body, glancing across the full slope of her breasts in an almost offhand manner.

He reached down with his free hand to encourage her partially separated thighs farther apart.

Her head snapped up. "Trev…"

"Close your eyes."

She reluctantly obeyed, also allowing her legs to part wantonly as the firm touch of the spray — feeling much like a questing finger — worked its way lower still. Target reached, the pulse hit squarely on her clit, almost sending her flying off the seat. Trevor moved the water back and forth, strumming across her rapidly engorging nub in a random pattern that left her gasping for air.

"Eyes closed."

She hadn't realised she'd opened them, hadn't been able to focus on anything, but willingly followed the directive without delay as the tension coiling within her zoomed past anything bearable.

Tipping over the edge in a supernova of pleasure, she arched and writhed, coming as hard as she could ever remember as colours flew behind her lids. This time, when she squirmed away from the spray, it immediately turned to a gentle, caressing shower.

She sensed Trevor replacing the showerhead then gave herself over to his strength as he gathered her still uncoordinated form to his, his erection pressing unabated against her hip. The water ceased and she finally opened her eyes to meet his heated chocolate gaze.

"Wow," she breathed, still trying to get her heart rate under control. The exhalation ended on a slight laugh. "I'm so glad I gave you a key."

"Oh, you can still talk?" he parried. "I must not've done my job." He walked her around the corner of the open shower onto the soft bathmat and grabbed a couple of towels. After drying himself in his normal slap-dash manner, he took his time drying her off, then swept her off her feet and carried her into the bedroom.

"Now, let's see if I can make you speechless."

Erica's orgasm hadn't left her sated—it had merely amped up her need to the point where she ached to have Trevor inside her. "Speechless sounds like it might take some doing. You know that I talk for a living, right?" Erica had worked hard to get where she was—a reporter for a large city network affiliate—and shy and retiring were definitely not character traits in that line of work. It was one of the things that had initially attracted her to Trevor. He was a comfortable choice for her, as they had similar personalities. Probably not the perfect choice, though, since they tended to burn hot and long together, wanting to *go-go-go* until they crashed with predictable fiery results.

"Hmm, a challenge. I love those." And he did. He was competitive that way. She didn't mind using a big of psychology to get him going. He tossed her lightly onto her bed then crawled up over her with the sinuous strength and grace of a large jungle cat, his muscles bunching and flexing.

God, he was beautiful. Almost too beautiful.

"I love it when you look at me that way." He nuzzled lightly alongside her breast, abrading her with his whisker growth but not quite touching her puckered nipple. She shifted in frustration then grabbed his head to direct him where she wanted him to go. He sucked the bud between his lips then smiled around her flesh as he lightly scored her with his teeth.

"Fuck. What way?" She was starting to lose track of the conversation. All of her focus was on the man laving her sensitive breasts in turn. He would be leaving marks, she could tell, and they both knew how much of a turn-on it would be for her to look at the results tomorrow in the mirror. "Careful. I might have to wear something with a low neckline this week."

He obligingly moved from her cleavage and turned his attention to the vulnerable, pale flesh of the side of her breast, near her underarm.

A giggle burst from between her lips. "Stop that!" She squirmed as he pinned her down and worked his way from her ribs to her hip bone. Her mouth went dry as he flashed a hot glance up at her from under his lashes. "Oh yeah." She thrust her pelvis up as much as she could with him still restricting her movements.

Trevor shook his head chidingly. "Still talking I see. I think I need to change tactics here."

She moaned as he left her pussy untouched and knee-walked up over her body until he was straddling her chest and arms. He slowly stroked his length a few times before tracing her lips with his cock head.

Erica flattened her tongue and opened her mouth invitingly. He groaned. "Fuck, that's hot."

She raised her head enough to take him in and ran her hands up his thighs to his extremely tight ass cheeks, cupping one in each hand to urge him forward.

He gently fucked her mouth as she worked her tongue around him, loving the heaving of his chest as he watched every move. Trev was extremely visual and she tapped into that in their bedroom play. She was used to being on-camera and aware of how she looked, as was he, so when they turned up the effort for each other, it was way hotter than any porn she'd ever seen.

A burst of salty pre-cum on her tongue and his increasingly taut facial expression signalled an end to the playful side of things. She knew from past experience he would need to be inside her any second. As soon as that registered, he pulled out and manhandled her on to her hands and knees.

The crinkle of a wrapper hit her ears as she waited and Erica smiled in satisfaction. It was going to be a fun ride. "Any day now," she taunted. She was wet with anticipation to the point where she could feel it on her pussy lips.

Without fanfare, he plunged into her, taking her breath away. "How's that?"

"Good," she managed.

"Just good?" He set up a rhythm that had her panting to keep up and thinking she might have to start working out harder. Trev adjusted her position a few times to perfectly fit his needs, and hers. He was the most incredible lover she'd ever had. His self-awareness of his body and its potential definitely translated to him using it to full effect.

"Very good?" Physically, things between them couldn't get better. If only their emotional connection carried the same weight.

Damn it.

She shut off her brain and gave herself over to the sensations coursing through her. He rested one hand on her lower back, just teasing at the top of her crack, and reached under with the other to use her slickness to stroke her clit. Just that little bit was enough to send her tightly-wound body hurtling over the edge.

She gasped as she came hard. Trevor swept her knees out from under her so she was lying flat on the mattress, then he sped up his thrusts a handful of times until he groaned.

"Oh God, yeah." He held her tight against him as he joined her in completion then rocked slowly in and out, prolonging the sensations for them both. He ended up curled over and around her protectively, lightly kissing her ear, her neck, her hair.

She closed her eyes and enjoyed his attentions. His body was an increasingly heavy weight atop hers and she wriggled until he got the hint and shifted to the side, pulling out. He lay there for a moment then rallied to stand and go back into the bathroom to clean up and dispose of the condom.

She heard the shower come on and knew he would make it a quick one—he liked to go to bed clean, something she agreed with completely. Erica managed to roll over and used the momentum to carry her to standing. She went straight to the shower and entered. Trev shifted to allow her to join him under the water for a quick rinse. No shenanigans this time, both of them just efficiently cleaning up.

"Done?" he asked and she nodded so he turned off the taps and they got out, dried off then went back to bed.

Erica stripped back the covers and they climbed in, each on their own side. She settled back to try to calm her mind, to pause it enough to sleep.

Trev assumed his usual sleeping position on his stomach and she turned her head on her pillow to smile at him. *He must be exhausted.*

His voice emerged from his pillow as a low rumble. "See? Speechless."

Erica had to laugh. She was tempted to say something just to instigate, but let it go so he could get some rest. Instead, she patted his sheet covered ass then turned on her side away from him.

He soon settled into sleep, as evidenced by his rhythmic breathing, but she lay there for a long time after, trying in vain to reconcile their relationship in her mind.

Awake with only her thoughts to keep her company, Erica finally gave up on getting her turbulent brain reined in enough to sleep. She slipped carefully from the bed, giving a heavily sleeping Trevor one last fond perusal before stifling a sigh and padding naked to her closet.

She eyed her 'comfort' robe and some warm slippers before admitting that it wasn't just a quick cup of tea she was going downstairs for. After dressing instead in yoga pants and a long-sleeved tee, she grabbed some wool socks and tucked them in her pocket, then descended to the kitchen to fix her drink. The cool wood floor under her feet reminded her autumn was here and bitterly, she couldn't help but equate that with her own declining fertility.

Not much time left.

Tonight, as always, Trevor had made sure he used protection, driving home the fact that he was not ready for a family. Was adamantly against it. The fleeting thought had occasionally crossed her mind that one of these times the condom might fail, but only in the depths of her secret hopes. Hope that what she'd found with Trevor would somehow morph from a committed relationship into something more long-term. Hope that she would somehow conceive without having to move on and use the final resort she had resisted for so long. Hope that Trevor would change his mind…before it was too late.

Hope he would give to her what he'd once been willing to give to anyone who chose him.

As she sipped her tea, she punished herself with the memories of her first meeting with Trevor and the hopes she'd once had.

Chapter Two

Five months earlier

"I'm telling you, you have no time to lose. Statistics aren't pretty for gals our age." Her friend Rhonnie leant forward and braced her elbows on the table. Her café-au-lait complexion thankfully looked a lot less sallow now that her morning sickness had passed. "If you don't have a friend-with-bennies you can ask to do it, you'll have to do the sperm bank thing." She reapplied herself to her mac and cheese.

Erica shuddered as she pushed back an errant lock of hair and looked at her once-appealing Chinese chicken salad. She wished she could trade—that cheesy mess looked really awesome, actually. "It gives me the willies thinking about the kind of guys who donate to something like that. Ego-maniacs with delusions of populating the earth, or guys who can't get dates on their own and live vicariously through the thought of women dosing themselves with their sperm. No thanks!"

"Ouch, that's harsh. I was perfectly willing to go that route if Barry hadn't stepped up to the plate. Well, figuratively anyway." Rhonnie's eyes sparkled at her as she took a sip of her herbal iced tea.

Erica found herself giving a reluctant smile at the humorous thought of her lesbian neighbour having actual sex with her gay best friend.

"And you're straight," Rhonnie continued. "You can get it hand-delivered, so to speak."

Erica snorted and irritatedly flipped her hair back once more before scrounging through her handbag for a clip. It was breezy today in the outdoor café they had met for lunch and she happened to be sitting with the wind at her back. "Hand-delivered." She snickered. "It's not actually the hand that does the trick, Rhon."

"Well, you know I don't have much experience with the body part that does." Rhonnie tried to look serious and they both ended up laughing.

Erica continued to fruitlessly search through her purse for something to pull her hair back with. If she didn't need it long enough to look decent on-air, she'd chop it all off. Finally giving up, she stood and started moving all her lunch items to a different seat. She was scooting over to the better positioned chair when a deep voice intruded from behind her.

"Pardon me, ladies. Do you mind if I join you?"

Erica turned her head just as she sat and looked up to see a tall, rugged dark-haired man standing behind the chair she'd just vacated.

She exchanged puzzled looks with Rhonnie, who shrugged and nodded.

"Sure." Erica indicated the empty chair, giving the stranger an appreciative once-over as he sat. "I'm Erica, and this is Rhonnie."

"Trevor," he introduced himself then settled back, totally comfortable, as though he chatted with complete strangers every day. On closer inspection, he looked younger to Erica than he'd first appeared, perhaps in his twenties. Though he was tanned, he didn't have any crinkling going on at the corners of his eyes yet.

"Sorry to intrude on your lunch, but I couldn't help overhearing your conversation about sperm donors."

"Oh God." Erica closed her eyes as she thought back on what she'd said. Her face flamed, then she pinched Rhonnie under the table as she heard her friend laugh.

"It's okay. I just wanted to give you some insight. You see, I've been a donor."

Erica's eyes flew open and she again ran her gaze over the gorgeous, muscular man, not missing one positive attribute, from his warm brown eyes, to his naturally wavy, full head of dark brown hair, to his very fit form. No glasses either. "You're a sperm donor?" she asked incredulously.

A little part of her mind was rubbing its hands together in glee. *He's perfect*, it whispered to her. *Sign me up. For the 'hand-delivery' option, please.*

Rhonnie laughed yet again and Erica shot her an irritated glance. Bad enough she was pregnant—now she was laughing at her? Rhon was so off her speed dial.

"So I take it you don't fall into either the ego-maniacal or the dateless-loser category?" Rhonnie asked innocently.

"Not last time I checked," he teased back as he turned his amused gaze on Erica.

Wishing the earth would just swallow her up, Erica gritted her teeth and put on a semblance of a self-deprecating smile while she waited for the duo to stop laughing together as if *they* were the old friends.

"Seriously," Rhonnie directed at Trevor, who looked completely at ease with the whole situation. Erica was forced to admire his self-confidence and personable nature. "Why would you ever donate to a sperm bank?"

Trevor met the question calmly. "My brother and I were fathered by a donor. And I really have no desire to ever be a parent myself, but I believe in the system, so I thought, why not?"

Erica's eyes widened in shock. Trevor's mom had apparently hit the donor jackpot.

Rhonnie frowned slightly. "How could you donate if you didn't know your paternal information? That's all protected, right?"

He grinned. "Works just fine when it's the same sperm bank."

Rhonnie nodded as if considering. "Which one did you use?"

Erica leant forward in anticipation of the answer to Rhonnie's million-dollar question.

He named one well known to them both, one they'd even discussed as a possibility for Erica—Rhonnie had done plenty of research before she made the decision to go with Barry as the father of her child. Excitement built in Erica as she wondered at the kismet that he brought Trevor past their table while they'd been talking about this topic.

Then he crushed the newly budding germ of a plan in Erica's head by adding, "But I've withdrawn my donations from public use."

"Why?" Erica and Rhonnie chorused, and Trevor looked uncomfortable for the first time.

"It's a long story." He almost looked as though he was considering sharing, then Erica saw the veil come down. "Personal reasons." His tone made it clear there would be no more information forthcoming. After a brief awkward pause, he continued, "But when I overheard what you were discussing so passionately, I still felt as though I should reassure you that the system is a good one and can be the right choice if you're looking at it for solid reasons."

Rhonnie nodded. "That's what I keep telling her." She ran her hand over her almost non-existent baby bump. "I actually have a friend who donated for mine."

Trevor grinned. "So I heard, and with no hand-delivery, even." His eyes sparkled with humour as Rhonnie finished shovelling a bite of her lunch into her mouth and coughed out a laugh. "Congratulations."

The waiter came over and Trevor ordered a chipotle steak wrap and ice water without consulting the menu.

Rhonnie's eyebrows went up. "Do you eat here often?"

He shrugged. "Not as frequently as I used to."

"Oh?" Rhonnie bristled slightly and Erica braced herself. Rhonnie was the restaurant's manager and understandably biased to love her baby. That said, she knew Rhon didn't mind constructive feedback. She just hoped that Trevor was nice about it.

"I'm out of town a lot and I need to keep my boyish figure for my job. So, depending on my schedule, I either can't indulge or I'm rolling through at odd hours."

"Boyish figure, huh." Erica sat back and gave him a long assessment. "Doesn't look all that boyish from where I sit," she flirted.

Trevor wasn't in the least embarrassed by her intense perusal, grinning appealingly back at her. If anything, he seemed to welcome it. "What I mean is, I use my body to make my living, so I have to watch the unnecessary calories."

"What is it you do? Actor?" Rhonnie queried. Her plate was empty and she was eyeing Erica's salad. Becoming accustomed to her friend's ravenous appetite, she shoved it over and silently indicated for her to help herself.

"Not exactly. I'm a fitness model and demonstrator, so I do print and video."

Rhonnie immediately pulled out her iPhone and Googled him. She scrolled through the images.

"Wow, look at some of the magazines you've scored covers for!"

Erica found herself peering over Rhonnie's shoulder at the bounty his currently clothed state only hinted at, and her one-track mind gave her another pointed nudge at the genetics on display.

The waiter brought Trevor's meal and more bread for Rhonnie. As the others ate, Erica found herself relaxing in his company. They continued the conversation when Trevor asked the ladies about their respective occupations. Trevor gave Erica an intense once-over when she admitted to her career with their city's major-market network affiliate, but the barrage of questions and fawning she sometimes received never materialised. Instead he only commented that he'd thought she looked familiar, and moved on to question Rhonnie about her own work.

"Ah! No wonder you were so worried when I said I didn't come here often."

Rhonnie blushed. "Guilty. I'm glad you like it. And we do have some really healthy things on the menu." She waved a fork at Erica's salad. "But if there's something in particular you'd like to see, I can try to get it on the menu for you."

Trevor cocked his head. "That's very nice of you. Thank you. And really, a few more high protein, low carb options could only be a win-win in this city with so many body conscious people."

They talked for a while longer. Between the two gregarious people talking now about food and diet, Erica just listened while she sipped at her drink. Trevor was a lot of fun to be around and very easy on the eye, and she was reluctant for the surprise lunch date to end.

Eventually Trevor set his napkin to the side of his plate and stood. He pulled out his wallet and tossed down a twenty. "I have to get going, ladies. Rhonnie" — he grasped her hand — "good luck with the rest of your pregnancy." Then he turned to Erica and his smile increased in wattage. Feeling a bit foolish for her lack of participation in the conversation, she prepared to say goodbye.

Instead, Trevor surprised the life out of her by inviting her to dinner the following night.

* * * *

Now, five months later, they were dating exclusively and had keys to one another's condo. The sex was amazing, the conversation flowed, and their relationship didn't seem to suffer during each of their frequent absences for work. In fact, Trevor was pretty much perfect in her mind. Except for one major detail.

He laughed at the idea of ever wanting to have kids.

And her biological clock was more like Big Ben right now.

Was it selfish to want to break up with the perfect guy just so she could — what? — search randomly for Mr Ready-to-be-a-Dad?

Of all the crappy timing…

"Tick-tock," she muttered, tears pricking her throat.

Chapter Three

Erica managed to ignore Trevor's ringtone until it went to voicemail yet again, trying unsuccessfully to tune it out by reviewing her notes for the voiceover she was about to record.

You are such a coward.

She was, and she knew it. But for the life of her, she couldn't bring herself to begin the *we're-in-different-places* conversation with Trevor, even though she'd rehearsed it at least a hundred times.

Every time Trevor went out of town on a shoot or publicity gig, she told herself she would break it off as soon as he got home. And every time he returned, she saw that brilliant, familiar smile directed at her and wimped out.

Coming up on six months of dating, she could feel herself getting in deeper and deeper. In fact, without the obstacle of her obsession with having a child and his adamant—yet honest, she grudgingly admitted—refusal to go there, she might have even been considering popping the question to him at this point. They were obviously well-matched despite the age difference, and there was love between them. Not the passionate, dramatic love of cinema, but a steady, pleasing, and somehow more *real* feeling love than she had ever imagined.

Waging an inner war and losing to her curiosity, Erica finally caved and listened to the two-day series of voicemails from Trevor.

"Hi babe. Been a long day here, and no cell reception where we were, so finally have a chance to check in. Hope you're doing good. I'll call you tomorrow."

"Hey, it's me. It's beautiful here, you should really come along with me one of these times. Meanwhile, it looks like I might be home a couple of days early. Something's come up, and luckily the stars aligned and I was able to convince the photographer to wrap my part of the shoot today in one really long day rather than having to hang around until Wednesday. So I'll be seeing you soon. Love you."

"Hi. Hope everything's okay. I keep missing you. Anyway, I'm flying stand-by and looks like I'll be getting on this flight, so I'll be home late tonight. Can't wait to see you. I have a surprise for you, too, and also something to ask – something I've been thinking about for a while now." He cleared his throat. *"So…I'll see you tomorrow."*

Erica paused with her finger on the key to erase the last message and instead hit replay, listening with growing concern. A surprise? And something to ask?

Oh crap. Was *he* going to pop the question?

Breaking into a sudden, sickening sweat, she tried to think of what else he could have possibly meant by that sort of uncharacteristically hesitant mention. Trevor was nothing if not confident. But the nervousness in his voice had come through loud and clear. Whatever it was, it was big.

Pulling the Scarlett act again, she firmly turned her mind away from Trevor and back to the job at hand.

* * * *

After spending the rest of her day being surprisingly productive, buried in the depths of her to-do list, Erica finally gave up on working when she found herself drifting off for the third time in as many emails. The world outside the windows was dark and her assistant, Miranda, looked bushed.

"Why don't you head out? I'm wrapping up anyway," Erica called to Miranda, and received only a half-hearted wave in response.

Youch. She definitely has a Starbucks card coming for putting up with my crap.

She gathered her things and headed for the door, scrolling through her texts. Nothing from Trevor, so he probably hadn't landed yet. He was good about letting her know when he was on the ground.

Alone in her car with only her thoughts for company, it was impossible to keep her mind from circling back to the conundrum she found herself in. Suddenly not wanting to go back to her empty condo, she dialled Rhonnie.

"What's up, girlfriend?" came the greeting over the car's speakers.

"Well, I was going to ask if you were working, but the background noise answers that question." The din of the pub was unmistakable. "You guys busy tonight?"

"Very, but I'll snag you a table if you're coming by."

Erica smiled with gratitude. "Thanks. I'll be there in ten." She sat up a bit straighter in the driver's seat of her Audi.

Not sure whether she was using the dinner outing to escape or confront her dilemma, she debated about whether to even raise the discussion with Rhonnie, right up until she actually saw her friend's face and suddenly found herself fighting back tears.

Rhonnie's welcoming smile morphed into a look of concern. She took Erica by the elbow, leading her to a somewhat isolated pub table back by an order station. Whispering a drink order to the waiter on the way past, she guided Erica onto one of the stools and immediately sat across from her.

"Okay, spill it. What's wrong?"

"You're busy," Erica hedged, not sure if she wanted to get into it at all, but the sympathetic face was implacable. She took a deep breath. "I'm going to break up with Trevor."

Just the slightest frown was her friend's only reaction as she met her gaze steadily, evidently waiting for more information.

"It's just that..." Erica found herself wanting to tell Rhonnie everything. "It hit me recently that while I do love Trevor, it's not love-love. I could totally see us together for the long-haul, but there just something...missing."

Rhonnie nodded sympathetically. Their iced teas arrived and Erica tried to compose her thoughts while taking a few sips without really tasting it.

"He's been gone on a shoot, and I've been totally ducking his calls."

"Did he get upset?"

"No, just the opposite. He continued to leave messages as his normal cheerful self...well, until today."

"What did he say?"

Erica shook her head, not sure why she was so upset by the thought of having to turn Trevor down if he did propose. "Well, it's hard to— Oh, here...I'll just play it." She pulled out her phone and went to voicemail, then replayed his final cryptic message from today. Afterward, she looked at Rhonnie, troubled. "Am I jumping to conclusions that he might be thinking about popping the question? What else could he want to ask me that would make him sound so nervous? Something that he's been thinking about for a while?" She dropped her head onto her hands. "I just don't know what to do. I don't want to lose Trevor, but..."

"But you're at different places in your lives."

"Yes." Then she shocked both herself and Rhonnie by adding, "I think I'm ready to look at AI with a donor."

The decision seemed to well up out of nowhere, but it felt right, much more so than the pipe dream of trying to magically find the right man she could love *and* who wanted kids, right now.

"That's great, but why do I get the feeling you think Trevor and getting inseminated are mutually exclusive? Have you guys talked about this?"

Erica gratefully accepted a refill of her glass of tea from the waiter and waited for him to leave before answering. "Not specifically, but he's so young. And the larger point is, he's not ready to be a parent, even if the baby's not his. I don't know if he'll ever be, and"—she paused, looking down at her fingers, toying with the napkin—"I can't start this process knowing he's not going be there for the end result. And I can't wait." She looked up and met Rhonnie's glistening eyes. "I'm forty-four, Rhon. If I don't do this now, it's not going to happen."

"Maybe he'll surprise you, hon. I think you should tell him what you want to do."

Erica shook her head, frustrated. "Every time the subject has come up, even peripherally, even that first day—you were there," she reminded her friend, "he just clams up and gets this really set look on his face. Whatever his reasons are—for not wanting to be a dad, for withdrawing his specimens—they are obviously deep and real and not up for discussion." She shrugged resignedly. "I guess more than anything that should tell me we're not right for each other, that he can't just tell me why he's so adamant about it. He has to know my interest in the topic, but he avoids it like the plague. Always distracts me with sex," she grumped, then met Rhonnie's eyes, and suddenly they were both laughing.

"Well, he does," she defended, then chuckled, her mood lightening with the hilarity, even though it felt a bit hysterical on her part. "I'm going to do it tonight. He'll be back from his trip, and I…" She straightened her shoulders as the certainty of her decision gave her some inner strength. "I can't put it off. It's not fair to either of us, and besides, after his message today, I think he's getting more serious about me than he should. It's time."

Rhonnie touched her hand comfortingly. "You know I'm here for you no matter what." She sat back up. "Are you going over now? Do you want some dinner first?"

Erica grimaced. "No, I don't think I can eat."

But Rhonnie insisted, and as a compromise, Erica ended up leaving with a wrap in a to-go container.

She pulled into Trevor's condo complex on the waterfront, found an outdoor guest parking spot and removed his garage door opener from her sun visor with a sigh. Might as well make a clean break, and give him back his keys tonight too. Giving her phone a glance to confirm that, no, he still hadn't called, she debated what to do. Not wanting to spend any extra time hanging out in his condo—somehow it just felt wrong to be in there alone given her decision—she instead found a bench overlooking the water and mechanically ate her sandwich in the dark.

Another half-hour went by and, getting chilled, she finally succumbed to the lure of Trev's warm apartment, letting herself in for the last time. It was quiet and dark. She flipped on the entry light, then paused, startled, as she reached to hang his key and opener on the hall tree hook.

Keys on the entry table. And a pair of black loafers kicked haphazardly to the side.

He's home?

Erica froze now that the moment was upon her. She must have stood there in the hall for ten minutes, fighting with herself on whether to slip out or walk down to his bedroom.

You are so weak, she chastised herself as her feet led her down the hall, tracing the path she had walked so many times with the man she was about to say goodbye to.

You can talk in the morning. What's one last night in his arms?

Unable to find an acceptable answer to that, she barely paused at the bedroom door, instead continued inside to find Trevor sprawled out on his bed. His suitcase, unopened, was off to one side, and an untidy pile of clothes were at her feet. He'd evidently just stripped and climbed into bed, exhausted. He must really have been tired if he hadn't even taken a shower. Her gaze softened as she looked her fill, wishing it could be different. He was in his customary sleeping position on his stomach, hugging his pillow, sheet covering him just to the hips and one leg cocked up. Trevor didn't snore, but his breathing was audible, heavy and rhythmic.

Not worrying about waking him—he always slept like the dead—Erica took a quick shower to rinse off, then slid into bed next to him. His warm, sleeping scent tickled her nose, and her body began to react, her pussy tingling with anticipation.

Stop it. Time to sleep, not get off.

Trevor's shoulders were cool to the touch, so she drew the sheet and comforter up over them both and tucked herself up against him, her back to his side. Even with tomorrow's confrontation looming over her, Erica took comfort in his warming presence, and soon felt herself drifting into sleep.

Chapter Four

Colin was dreaming.

And it was one he was going to hate to wake up from.

The almost-forgotten feeling of blood pooling, tightening his groin, was a huge relief but made it feel almost unbearably sensitive. He could feel every drag and cling of skin on skin as he thrust against the pillowy softness cradling his erection. Sliding his hand, he mapped a curvy, warm form, lost in the sensation of arousal, something he hadn't experienced for so long.

Since the accident.

His libido took a brief dip at that thought, but he shoved it away and continued to explore.

Feminine whispers—*I love you. I want you*—brought his rising passion ebbing back almost to reality once again. For what woman could love or want him after what had happened? Now that he was less than a man?

Then moist warmth engulfed his cock, driving every thought from his head and he arched into the heady feeling. Hands, petite but strong, anchored his hips, and he had to content himself with small pelvic rocks as he tangled his fingers into silky curls.

"Yes," he groaned, encouraging his phantom lover and she responded by increasing the slow suction along his shaft to sweat-inducing pressure. Pausing at his tip, her tongue glided around his sensitive cap before engulfing him once again.

One hand left his hips, only to grip his straining cock at the base, pumping him in time with the motion of her mouth on him. The other hand slid down the line of his inner thigh, and continued onward towards his groin. Part of his brain began to protest, but the slight edge of teeth along his shaft seized his whole attention, and he cried out in pleasure.

The sound seemed to echo in the room, and Colin opened his eyes, just as his dream lover—who was *real*, not a dream—cupped his sac.

And gasped in shock.

Her head popped up and he got his first look at his flesh-and-blood bed partner in the dim light of the room. Disbelieving brown eyes met his from under tousled auburn waves, and her full lips were parted, slightly puffy from the efforts of her prior attentions.

This observation brought him back to the reality of her hand still grasping his cock—his *erect* cock, wonder of wonders. His eyes slipped past her to see his brother standing at the foot of the bed, cupping his own erection through his pants, a slight smile on his face. Colin raised his eyebrow, but he decided to wait until later to lecture Trev about the weirdness of apparently hiring a hooker for him. The fog of his arousal and jet-lag combined to make it seem like a good idea to disregard all his wonderment—*who is she?* and *thank God, my cock still works!* — and return to the rapidly fading moment.

His head fell back and he thrust into her hand, and for a moment, she reflexively stroked his length.

"Trevor, what on earth happened?" Her voice was cultured and melodic. Not a pro, then.

And she thinks you're Trev.

"Your, um… Something's wrong with your balls," she continued. "I think one's hiding."

Colin opened his eyes as he fought a mirthless snort, and he looked into her concerned face then back at Trevor, whose lips twitched as he reached out to rest his hand on her lower back.

"Erica…"

She screamed and scrambled onto Colin's lap, and he automatically put his arms around her. She looked back over her shoulder then jolted, shock transmitting itself as every inch of her tensed at once. Erica was Trevor's current girlfriend, Colin remembered from his brother's emails, the one he wanted to move in with. Well, maybe not *girl*. She was definitely all woman.

His eyes roamed downwards, helpless to keep from appreciating her curvy form fully on display and pressed against him. Chivalry was *not* his strong suit at the moment.

"Trev?" she questioned as she looked back and forth between the two men.

She carefully separated herself from Colin and drew up the sheet, apparently realizing the ball-less wonder wasn't who she thought he was. But hadn't she arrived with Trevor? His travel-fuzzed brain, still back in China, couldn't begin to puzzle this out.

Trevor knee-walked across the bed to cradle her in his arms. "I'm sorry, sweets. I didn't mean to scare you." His gaze met Colin's over the top of her head, and he reached out a hand to briefly clap his brother's shoulder in silent greeting.

The identity of the 'intruder' settled, she gazed frankly at Colin, her sharp eyes examining every facet of his appearance, shaking her head slightly more than once. Her eyes dropped to his lap, and he followed her gaze to his groin, where his rampant erection hadn't yet caught up with the change in program. The depressingly deflated look of his right ball sac started to do the trick, though, and he sighed as he covered up.

Ah well. So much for finally getting there.

Trev spoke into the quiet. "Erica, I know this…is a lot to ask, and I promise I'll explain everything later, but how would you feel about continuing what you were doing?"

Of all the things Trevor could have said just then, that was by far the most unexpected. Erica couldn't see a trace of jealousy on his face, which puzzled her. Maybe she'd misjudged his feelings towards her.

She was facing the man on the bed next to her—obviously Trevor's twin—so she saw the flash of heat followed by his grimace in reaction to Trevor's question. And just before he looked away, she caught a tinge of regret or sadness in his eyes. It touched something inside her. Although it wasn't pity she felt just then, it was obvious that something had happened to him, and she paused in empathy, with the automatic denial still on her tongue.

On her tongue… She couldn't help but remember the warm weight of him in her mouth, Colin's cries of pleasure, the bitter-sweet taste of his pre-cum hitting her taste buds. While Trevor had been obviously appreciative when she'd gone down on him, his brother's strong, uninhibited reactions to her efforts had been flattering and arousing.

His brother. Oh God, what's his freaking name? Colby? Corey?

Colin, she remembered with relief.

Then he was moving away, seemingly resigned to leaving the couple in peace, and before she could think any further about the ramifications of her actions, she automatically grabbed his arm to stop his retreat.

His deep brown eyes, so familiar yet different in their depths, flashed to hers, measuring her with a defensive glare. "I'm not a charity case," he growled, but she noticed with feminine satisfaction he didn't move away, although he could have easily evaded her grasp.

And he was still hard.

She altered her grip so it was soothing, and she glanced at Trevor, seeing nothing but encouragement in his expression. No pressure, though. He was evidently going to let her make this decision for herself. She would find out later what his real reason for this was. In fact, he looked smug enough that if she didn't know better, she'd think he'd set her up. But to have arranged to have his brother in his bed and guess that she might come over and crawl in? Nope, no way he could have pulled that off.

She turned back to Colin, still and inscrutable as he waited for her reaction.

A ménage. Why not? she thought. *We're all adults, and it's not like it'll be awkward afterwards since Trevor and I are all but over.* The memory of why she'd come here was a sobering one, and it must have been reflected in her face because both brothers reacted, Trevor with a frown of concern and Colin with renewed determination to leave the bed. She smacked his firm ass with her hand as he began to turn away.

A charity case, huh? "No, you're not, but you *are* touchy," she retorted, and both brothers froze. Trevor moved first, his mouth twitching with amusement as she continued, "I don't do pity fucks, either, so it'll work out just fine to get together. If you're up for it."

Colin's jaw dropped, and she took advantage of his cessation of movement to lean forward and press a kiss to his parted lips. For long moments, they were still under her own, and she began to think his pride was going to make this impossible. His eyes searched hers from close proximity then squeezed closed. When his response finally came, it took her breath away.

Almost off-balance anyway with the effort to reach Colin's mouth, it took no effort at all for him to encourage her to twist and fall the short distance to the mattress. Taking control of the kiss, Colin landed on top of her and pressed her down into the mattress. He stroked his tongue into her mouth with an assurance she immediately responded to.

"God, you taste good," he murmured, and the sound of his voice—so like his brother's—reminded her of the unusual situation she had somehow fallen into. She raised her head to attempt to meet Trevor's eyes, but Colin brought her attention fully back to him by deepening the kiss to a lush, carnal mating.

"Don't think. Just feel," he demanded then trailed his lips down her throat, making her arch to encourage his exploration. His hands weren't still, trailing lightly across her arms, down and back up, then across her collarbone. His mouth had almost met up with his fingertips when he changed direction and licked and bit his way towards the full side of her breast, avoiding the taut peak. Erica groaned her frustration, even as she relished the seduction.

Finally free to look at Trevor, she watched as he bent towards her neck. "Hey," he whispered against her skin, his breath teasing at her nerve endings while his brother traced her ribs with his tongue. "Thanks for the awesome wake-up — even if it wasn't me."

"We're going to talk about that later, trust me," she warned without heat, then gasped as Colin and Trevor each latched onto a straining nipple and suckled in unison. "Oh God," she cried breathlessly, relishing the previously unknown sensation. "Have you two done this before?"

"Believe it or not, no." Trevor continued mouthing her breasts as he answered, while Colin shook his head, using the flat of his tongue to tease her peak. When he raked his teeth lightly across the sides, Erica squirmed — and thrust a hand between her own legs. She couldn't help it. She needed some pressure, something...

"Yeah. That's hot," Trevor praised in a husky voice, cupping behind one of her knees and pulling it back so she was ruthlessly exposed to their interested gazes as she pleasured herself.

"Oh, come on. Two young guys in this bed, I shouldn't have to be doing this to myself," she panted in frustration. Her brain was on vacation and every sense was attuned to what was happening with her body and their attentions.

As if in response, Colin tested her moist pussy with his fingers then began thrusting them inside, too shallowly to really ease her need, but enough to stretch her and make her want more. He slowly and deliberately jacked his hard, reddened cock in time with his fingering. Meanwhile, Trev arranged himself along her side and alternately soothed and plucked at her nipples while tonguing her ear and neck, seemingly content to let his brother solo.

The combination of Colin's shallow penetration with her practiced stimulation quickly became too much. He must have sensed her impending implosion because his rhythm became deep and purposeful as he fucked her with his fingers.

"Mmm." She couldn't take her eyes off him, watching his face strain as he focused on her. She was approaching the edge, but ached for him to be in her when she came. "Fuck me," she invited, needing more, wanting that big, beautiful cock inside her.

"Can I?" Colin's steady voice had a deep tone to it.

The question brought things to a halt for just a moment as it seemed to include both she and Trevor. Trev broke the standoff and reached back to the bedside table then handed his brother a condom, just as she responded, "Oh, hell yes."

Colin made short work of rolling it on and placing his cock head at her entrance. He shuddered as he began to push inside and she trembled in desperate response. The feel of his thick length pressing inexorably into her was heavenly, but it was the expression on his face that sent her against her known boundaries and beyond. He looked at her as if she held everything he'd ever searched for.

Simultaneously striving for the peak and wishing the build-up would never end, she surged with Colin until a particularly hard thrust sent her spiralling over the precipice and into a shattering climax. He rode her through it then stilled, coming with an almost silent groan as he held deep within her. Chest heaving, he braced himself above her, not once having lost eye contact, and she could almost feel a connection snapping into place between them.

Then he smiled and she caught her breath.

As Colin chuckled, his till-now serious expression lifted into a gorgeous grin. Her chest seized and she couldn't look away. She smiled in return, something inside her swelling with an unnamed emotion.

Oh no. No, no, no, she fruitlessly warned herself. *Don't you go falling for the other one now.*

Chapter Five

This time when Colin awoke he squinted at the clock but then had a hard time deciphering the shadows. Was it quarter after six in the morning or afternoon? This time of year, it was hard to tell. Rolling onto his back, he caught movement out of the corner of his eye—Trev, shifting around but still sleeping.

The whole crazy night suddenly came back to him.

Sex with Erica.

Sex…period…for the first time since the accident.

Yeah, but with Erica—Trevor's girlfriend. Who was nowhere to be seen.

Feeling a nearly uncontrollable urge to shake Trevor awake to talk, Colin instead took pity on him. Trevor had just got back from a long trip too, coming from the other direction. Smiling a little at his comatose brother, he pulled the covers up over him and went to take a long, hot shower. The night before he had barely rinsed off before collapsing into bed.

Trevor had told him his flight would be getting in late and had joked that whoever got there first got the bed. So when Colin had arrived at the condo before

Trev, he'd taken him at his word and had sleepily commandeered the bed.

Colin had just wrapped up two nearly consecutive year-long stints overseas. He'd gone ahead and sold his condo before he'd left for the first year, so was going to have to bunk in with Trev until he found a new place. Or he might just end up buying this one from Trev. Trev had mentioned he was going to sound Erica out about moving in together.

Finished with his leisurely soaping up, Colin shook his head as he began to shampoo his hair. He just couldn't figure the couple out. By all accounts, Trevor really cared for Erica, even using the word 'love'. But when Colin had teasingly pressed him about whether he was planning on popping the question, Trevor had said they wouldn't work out in the long run. And maybe there was something to that. Yes, the brothers had very different personalities, but Colin couldn't imagine sharing a woman he truly loved with another man, brother or not.

Guilt trip or not.

His hand made the familiar trip down to cup the empty side of his disfigured ball sac and he traced his fingertips along the scars. Trevor had nothing to feel guilty about, but Colin could still see the emotion in his eyes occasionally, and most of the time, he just let Trev do whatever made him feel better about it.

Offering up his girlfriend was way over the top, though, and it was time this all stopped. Especially now that they both knew Colin was functioning again. He would never father any children—he ignored the small twinge of regret that thought provoked—but at least he now knew he could have sex again. The thirteen months since the accident had gone by without a full erection, even partial ones fading once they passed a certain point.

Until last night.

No physical cause had ever been found, but the psychologist said it was performance anxiety, a normal by-product of the severe and disfiguring damage his genitalia had suffered in the accident. The accident Trevor was convinced was his own fault just because he'd been the driver, and because he'd been the one to demand that they go home instead of sucking it up and waiting out the rain.

If it was anyone's fault, it was Colin's for not putting the hastily packed tent bag in the back of the truck, instead of propping it on the passenger's side floor between his legs. No, it was no one's fault, just hydroplaning, but Colin knew if the situation was reversed, he would be just as likely to cling to guilt.

Bypassing his suitcase, he instead raided Trev's dresser and ended up with a long-sleeved T-shirt and what were likely Colin's own favourite sweatpants. Apparently, Trev had 'borrowed' them. Colin rolled his eyes and shot a mock-irritated glance at Trevor's still form.

Klepto.

Trev didn't even move while Colin rummaged through drawers to find socks. He unplugged his phone from the charger and found it was morning. A bit early, but he had to start adjusting to the time change sometime, and who knew how many hours he'd slept? The whole time and date change made the mental math impossible, especially before caffeinating.

Colin walked out to the kitchen, thinking to have some coffee and maybe try to find a newspaper, then stopped short at the sight of Erica perched on the counter stool, sipping her own steaming cup.

He paused to watch her for a moment before she noticed him. In the soft morning light, she made a pretty — if a bit pensive — sight, gazing at some distant spot out of the window, the slightest frown creasing her brow.

Wishing Trevor were here to smooth the way, but not wanting any time to go by before he made sure Erica wasn't having any morning-after regrets, he resumed walking into the room.

As she became aware of his presence, she opened her mouth to speak then narrowed her eyes. An unbidden grin came to Colin's face as he realised she was trying to figure out which brother he was.

"Morning, sweets," he teased as he crossed the room to confidently drop a brief kiss on her lips, before turning to make a beeline for the coffee maker.

"Morning, Colin," she returned and smirked at him.

He raised an eyebrow, a bit surprised she'd got it right so quickly. He put the coffee pod into the right compartment then pressed the start button. Nice that Trevor had gone more high-tech than the old school drip coffeemaker he used to have. "Okay, how'd you know?" He peeked in the fridge. *Score – half-and-half.*

Erica didn't look uncomfortable. Maybe she wasn't too freaked out about last night, after all. "Trevor quit drinking coffee a few months ago. Said he was tired of having to try to find good coffee on the road." A confirmed and happy addict, Colin shuddered at the thought as she continued, "I agree. Love it in the morning, myself. Plus, I know those are your sweats. He was pretty smug about swiping them, but he never really wore them, just hid them in his drawer."

I knew it. Once he had his coffee fixed, he took the other stool. "Nice investigative skills. You must be good at your job," he praised, leaning in a bit closer, enjoying her slight flush as she shifted.

She took a big drink of coffee before admitting, "To be honest, until you headed to the coffee machine, I wasn't sure. It's eerie—you look almost exactly alike. Well, with your clothes on," she added in a rush.

Ouch. Colin felt his smile drop at the reminder of his deformity. "Yeah, I guess it just takes one look below the belt to figure us out now," he muttered bitterly. He stood to go.

"No! Oh no, that's not what I meant. Crap." She reached out as though to catch him, distress all over her pretty face.

Not particularly wanting to continue the conversation, manners nevertheless made him stop when she tentatively touched his arm. He waited to hear what she thought might make up for a direct hit on a very sensitive topic for him.

"I wasn't even thinking about that. Just your builds. You know"—she rubbed his arm soothingly, and Colin found himself enjoying the touch despite his upset—"Trev has to keep up his über-muscles for his job. Not that you're not built," she hastily added then smacked her forehead twice with the flat of her free hand. "Fuck, nothing's coming out right. I'm usually a little more tactful than this."

The swear word had a smile tugging at his lips, that plus the fact that she seemed sincere about not having meant what he'd immediately jumped to conclusions about. "It's okay." He shrugged. "I shouldn't have assumed you meant the worst."

"No, seriously. I sound like an idiot." She was stroking his chest now, standing close, and damned if he wasn't enjoying it. But in the light of day, he had to remember she was Trev's girlfriend, not his. He took a step back and her hand fell away, as if she too had just realised what she was doing.

"Jesus, it's early. What the hell are you two doing up?" Trevor came around the corner bare-chested — with his 'über-muscled' torso on display — wearing a pair of silk sleep pants Colin had actually bought for him, intended to give to him as a gift.

Which had been still packed in his suitcase.

"You're welcome," he prompted sarcastically, waving a hand to indicate the pants. "Anything else in my stuff you need, just go ahead and help yourself."

"Thanks, I will." Trevor smiled wickedly and turned to greet Erica. "Hey, sweets, good morning." He gave her a lingering kiss, and Colin grew uncomfortable with the display. Why, he didn't know.

Yes, you do. Those sweats aren't the only thing green in here.

Relax, it's just because she's the first sex you've had in over a year.

Colin thought about that, and it made a sort of sense. Erica smiled at Trevor and rumpled his bed-tossed hair. They were the couple, and it looked as if they were one that shared a good rapport. Colin was the third wheel and nothing more. Now that it appeared things were working down there, he needed to get out and find someone not taken.

After one final kiss, Trevor finally let Erica up for air. "So, what did you think of my surprise?" He gestured to Colin, and Colin choked on the sip he was taking. *What?*

Erica's eyes went wide with shock and her mouth dropped open. "Sleeping with your brother was my surprise? You *planned* this?" she asked incredulously.

Colin shook his head to negate the idea, feeling relief at being able to infer from Erica's surprised reaction and questions that Trevor hadn't set last night up somehow. It had been beyond confusing to wake up and have them both there, but evidently she'd joined him in bed thinking that he was Trevor, who had arrived after the fact.

It hurt his brain to try to suss out. He took a large drink of coffee.

"What? No." Trevor frowned briefly, looking taken aback. "I mean, him moving back from Asia and you finally getting to meet him."

"Oh." Erica exhaled, sounding as relieved as Colin felt. "Yes" — she turned a brilliant smile on Colin — "I'm very glad to finally get…to know…him." She trailed off as the dual meaning hit her. Then the three of them laughed at the double entendre, and it looked to Colin like they might actually escape from the situation without too much lingering awkwardness. "Although you could have mentioned he was your twin. You always just said 'brother'. Not exactly full disclosure." She lightly socked his arm with a small fist.

"Ouch," Trev overreacted playfully, rubbing his triceps. "Well, honestly, I really don't think of him as my twin."

She raised a sceptical eyebrow, and Colin jumped in to defend his brother's point of view. "It's true. Mom didn't want us to be known as 'the twins', or have people think of us as a unit instead of individuals. So she purposely never used the term 'twins', and I guess it carried over."

"That's smart. She must be a very strong woman. And very lucky to have you both." A tinge of sadness shadowed her eyes.

Colin glanced inquiringly at Trevor and watched as Trevor stiffened and visibly withdrew.

What the hell? Some sore point there.

Before Colin could respond, Erica clapped her hands together as though to break the mood. "So!" She deliberately diverted the conversation, "If Colin was the surprise, what was the question you wanted to ask me? And it better not have been—'do you want to keep doing what you were doing?'" Her words were teasing, but the set of her shoulders betrayed her tension as she awaited Trev's answer.

"Ah. The question…" Trevor visibly turned up the charm in a way that Colin was all too familiar with. It was the way Trevor laid the groundwork for a big request or plan that he wasn't sure would go over well.

He shook his head. "Oh brother," Colin muttered under his breath, then put on an innocent look when the couple turned to look at him. "Don't mind me." He headed to the coffee machine to make a second cup, since he'd gone through the first mug in such a hurry.

"Well," Trevor began, "with Colin moving back and this place being so small… I thought since we were at each other's places overnight most nights we're in town anyway, I could maybe just move in with you. At least until Colin finds a place."

Colin watched Erica digest this, appearing to struggle to control her expression. "Hey," he chimed in, concerned about the warring emotions on her face. "I don't mind sleeping on the couch for a while. It's cool. Really."

Trev gave Colin a warning glance and he could read the intent just fine. *Keep out of it.*

"It'll be fun being roomies," his brother encouraged Erica. "So what do you say?"

Chapter Six

In the end, Erica couldn't do it.

Damn it – you are so weak.

So here she was the next morning, holding the door for Trevor and Colin as they made trip after trip back and forth between their cars and her condo with Trevor's things. She thought of it as holding the door rather than helping with the move because the two brothers had declined every offer to help other than that.

Surprisingly, Trevor had taken over the guest room rather than moving into her bedroom. She wasn't sure what to think about that, other than perhaps he felt guilty about pressuring her into acceding so he decided to make it more about accommodation rather than their relationship status.

It was somewhat of a relief.

The guys left to make a trip for 'one more thing', though for what, she wasn't sure. Trevor seemed to have more clothes than she did, and the guest room closet was already full, as was the dresser. They weren't moving any furniture since Colin would be using it, and similarly, most of his work-out and sports equipment would be staying there since there was no reason to move it right away.

Erica realised that she was thinking of this as a temporary thing and she hoped that Trevor's choice of bedroom meant he felt the same way. She wasn't sure how she would feel if he ended up expecting to sleep with her...

And what the hell was she thinking anyway? He was her boyfriend — why wouldn't he sleep with her?

She didn't like that Colin popped into her head. Not that she didn't like thinking about him — more that she found herself thinking about him too often.

Erica sighed and forced herself to go get ready for work.

* * * *

When she unlocked her front door later that night after a long day, she wasn't sure whether to expect Trevor to be there or not. She hadn't spoken to him all day, throwing herself into work to try to keep her mind off the myriad complications in her life.

She stepped inside and instantly smelt the heady scent of garlic and Italian herbs and...seafood? She was surprised...and immediately hungry. In fact, she was salivating like a dog. Italian was probably her favourite type of food, but one she didn't indulge in very often. The camera added pounds and pounds were exactly what she ate in pasta and bread when she gave in to temptation.

Trevor must have picked up takeout from Gino's or Carabba's or somewhere.

She smiled as she set down her purse, kicked off her heels then walked into the kitchen.

To her astonishment, it wasn't Trevor but Colin with his back to her. It was somewhat telling that she could already tell them apart at a glance. He was stirring something on the stove and the kitchen was a sort of controlled mess which proved that, far from takeout, this dinner was homemade.

Trevor walked in from the dining room holding a bottle of wine. "Are you sure I shouldn't chill—" He grinned when he saw her there. "Hi! Surprise! We made dinner for you as a thank you."

"We?" Colin turned around and raised an eyebrow at his brother, but he wore a smile.

"I got the wine," Trevor protested. "And I warmed up the... Oh crap, the bread!" He thrust the wine bottle into Erica's hands then opened the small, separate warming oven. After grabbing the edges of the foil with his bare hands and flinging it onto the nearest counter, he looked up at them and winked. "Perfect."

The toasted garlic bread did look good. Erica smiled back at him then at Colin, who was shaking his head. "You lead a charmed life." He banged the spoon on the side of the pan then set it down on a dish. "The pasta's drained, so we can dish out. I didn't see a big pasta serving platter..." He trailed off inquiringly.

"I have no idea what one of those would even look like." Erica wasn't exactly Susie Homemaker. In fact, she hadn't even realised she had a vegetable steamer, but Colin had opened the lid on one to reveal perfect looking broccoli. "How about we each just serve ourselves and carry our plates over?" she suggested.

Colin looked a bit disappointed but Trevor immediately grabbed the stack of three plates from the counter and distributed them to the others. Wanting to soothe Colin, she moved to his side and lightly bumped his arm. "This smells amazing. What did you make?"

"Just some linguine with clam sauce. It's one of my favorites and not exactly something I ate while I was in China. Plus Trevor told me you love pasta..." He took her plate from her hand. "Let me dish you out at least. Do you want to go change into some comfy clothes? I know we caught you just as you came in and...well..."

Erica looked down at her taupe suit and yellow silk blouse then at the sauce and grimaced. "Great idea. I'll be right back," she called over her shoulder as she hurried from the kitchen.

She walked into her bedroom and had the weirdest thought about whether she should close the door. It was odd having two other people in the place while she undressed, but then again, after all that had passed between them, it would be sort of prissy to get modest at this point.

"Arrgh," she growled, frustrated with the lack of control over her own life.

She left the door open and crossed to her walk-in closet. She loved its size, mostly because it was big enough to have room for her dressers so all of her clothes were in one place. More like a dressing room than just a closet. She even had a padded bench style seat to perch on to put on socks and stockings.

Erica shed her suit and top and added them to her dry cleaning bag then hurriedly chose a pair of jeans and a soft, dark blue T-shirt, which she placed on the bench before sitting down. She began to roll down one of her thigh highs then heard a sound and glanced up.

"Wow." Admiration shone in Trevor's eyes. He gestured for her to continue. "It's like walking into a movie boudoir." He winked. "I won't say what kind of movie."

She arched her eyebrow at him, fighting a smile. He was really just too charming for his own good and didn't need any encouragement. "Was there some reason you barged in here or were you just hoping to get a free show?"

"Hmm? Oh—wanted to see if you would like red or white wine with dinner. Colin said it's one of those meals that goes well with either so thought we'd give you the choice."

She finished the first stocking and started on the other. Erica could almost feel his gaze following her progress down her leg. A small, secret part of her wished that it had been Colin who had come to check on her and caught her undressing...but then, he wouldn't just walk into her bedroom unannounced like his brash sibling.

"What kind does Colin want? It's kind of his special meal." Erica stood and hesitated a moment then thought *what the hell* and unhooked her bra. As soon as the ambient air hit her warm skin, her nipples puckered.

She reached for her jeans and her breasts swayed heavily as she bent and straightened. A glance at Trevor revealed a sexy smile curving his mouth. After stepping into the legs, she wiggled herself into the fitted and well-worn jeans as Trevor leaned against the door jamb and unabashedly enjoyed the show.

"He chose red at first, then second-guessed himself. I think he really wants to impress you. He likes you."

Trevor stepped closer and trailed a finger down one taut bud, but his words were like a splash of cold water on her libido. Not only was there another person in the house, it was someone they had once included in their sex play and...and now what? Would they again? When she'd decided to roll with it, it had been with the knowledge that she and Trevor would be going their separate ways soon, but that hadn't happened. Now Erica felt a bit as though they were...cheating on Colin, though that was foolish. Wasn't it?

She grabbed her T-shirt and dragged it over her head and down, wordlessly cutting off any possibility of sex. With a rueful smile, Trevor shrugged good-naturedly and turned around to lead the way back to the kitchen. When they got there, Colin was nowhere to be seen.

She frowned as wild imaginings ran through her head. Had he come to see what the holdup was and seen them? Was he hurt or did he leave to give them privacy?

Just then he walked back into the room from the dining room and she exhaled in relief. What the hell had she been thinking? She'd been right the first time—Colin would never just walk into her room, and even if he saw something between Trevor and her, why would it bother him? They were the couple.

Guilt at her small fantasy pricked her and she found it hard to meet either of the men's eyes. Maybe she wasn't built to handle something like a ménage. No—actually it was more that she was already so unsettled about her and Trevor and their relationship that there was no foundation on which to base her emotional decisions at the moment. She and Trevor really needed to have a chat and soon.

She walked blindly into the dining room and stopped in surprise. A beautiful bouquet of colourful flowers sat in the middle of the table, framed by lit tapers. Three places were set and dished with food at one end of the rectangular table.

Colin smiled when she turned to him. He poured a glass of wine and held it out to her. She accepted it gratefully. "Thank you. This all looks beautiful."

"You're welcome. Have a seat." He set down his glass on the table and pulled out the chair at its head for her. After helping her, he took his own seat to her right and Trevor sat to her left, so they were an intimate tête-à-tête rather than spread out. It made sense, really.

"Eat while it's warm," Colin invited them. "Trev, can you pass the garlic bread?"

The food was delicious and Erica ate way too much, but just couldn't resist. How often did she get a home-cooked meal this wonderful? Hardly ever. She never really cooked for herself — it was just easier to pick something up or let Rhonnie feed her with her crazy hours. And Trevor had never shown much inclination to cook like this. His kitchen skills ran more along the lines of how he thought of food — as fuel, not a pleasure to be savoured. Colin, though, seemed to appreciate the entire sensory experience as well as the process.

When she questioned him about it, he smiled a bit self-deprecatingly at first, but soon warmed to his subject. "I'm a bit of a home-body — when I'm not off on a contract, that is — so last thing I want to have to do is go out for meals I could make myself."

"It's amazing. You're very talented," she praised him.

"Thanks. It's a pleasure." His pride showed when he continued, "I actually learned a lot while I was in China about Asian cuisine. I'd love to cook for you again sometime, show you what I've managed to pick up." He cleared his throat and glanced at his brother. "Both of you, of course."

"I'd love that," she answered honestly.

"Yeah, definitely. Maybe I should have stayed at the condo with you. I'd forgotten the benefits to living with you, man." Trevor leant back in his chair. "You'll just have to come here to cook for us like tonight. I mean," he added quickly, probably realising that Colin might not want to be arbitrarily volunteered for K-P, "we'll supply the wine and groceries then you can give it your magic touch." He paused then added in true Trevor fashion, "And you'd get to enjoy our company."

They all laughed. Erica was enjoying having both the brothers there in her home...and that was a huge quandary.

There was a very good chance that Colin could have been someone more her type than Trevor, but she'd met Trevor first. She was currently *with* him. No way could she even consider anything happening with Colin now. And even if she and Trevor called it quits, it would be the height of tacky to then start dating his brother. Talk about a daytime gossip show set-up.

On the other hand, if she broke it off with Trevor now as she'd planned, she wouldn't have any excuse to see Colin anymore, and the thought of him disappearing from her life made her a bit queasy. Either way, she was screwed, and not in the good way.

Lust after her boyfriend's brother? Or after her ex-boyfriend's brother?

Awful choice. Neither one was where she wanted to go with her life.

Fuck.

Why did she have to like Colin so damn much? And why couldn't she have met him first?

Damn it.

Chapter Seven

Beep.

"Fuck," Colin cursed as he stopped moving and let the machine carry him down. He had debated making the phone call for exactly an hour and still hadn't arrived at a firm decision. He knew it was an hour because it had been the entire time that he'd been on the elliptical in his brother's workout room.

He climbed off the machine and debated grabbing a towel to dry off with then decided to just take a shower instead. When he walked into the bedroom, he looked straight to the bed, thinking, as always, about the incredible night he'd shared with Erica there.

It was beyond frustrating that he'd found such an amazing and sexy woman…who was completely off-limits to him.

"Don't be so dramatic. Trev being with her isn't keeping you from being friends with her," he muttered. And that was the unkindest cut of all. Not only was he incredibly attracted to her, but he also *liked* her. Loved spending time with her. Speaking of which…

Might as well.

He stripped off his workout shorts and tossed them into the hamper then crossed to the dresser to pick up his phone. Before he could talk himself out of it, he quickly tapped to dial for Erica and waited.

"Hi, Colin." Erica sounded like she was smiling.

"Having fun?" he asked.

"Oh, kinda sorta not really. Been one of those days. But it's always good to hear from you. What's up?"

"I was just wondering if you wanted to have dinner tonight." Crap, that really sounded like he was asking her on a date. Oh well. So much for rehearsing the casual approach.

"Umm..."

Colin winced as she hesitated. "I totally get it if you're busy or if you feel weird without..."

"No, not at all. I'd love to. I'm just trying to figure out what time I might be done. I don't want you waiting on me."

Reassured by her sincere tone of voice, he relaxed a bit. "I don't have a timetable I need to stick to. Whenever works best for you. Would you rather go somewhere casual, or I could cook and we could eat in?"

A light sigh came over the line. "Eating in sounds great actually. I'm just really tired of people right now and being at home and quiet would be heavenly. But we could do take-out if it's too much hassle. I hate to make you do all that work for me."

Colin grinned at how fed-up she allowed herself to come across when she'd admitted she was sick of people. "Tell you what," he offered, thinking fast, "I'll fix something for dinner at my place instead and then bring it over to yours. That way you get a home-cooked meal and the peace of your own place, and you don't have a mess in the kitchen." He cut her next words out before she could get them out, "And yes, I'm sure. I wouldn't have asked otherwise."

She chuckled and the warm sound had an instantly arousing effect. It wasn't until his shaft began to slowly fill that he realised he'd been standing there talking to her while naked. He dropped his hand to cup his growing erection. Man, she was like the sex goddess of healing. He'd been stuck on 'off' for so long that he'd forgotten how good it felt to have a normal reaction to a sexy woman, much less the day to day ebb and flow of hormones.

"Okay, well if you're sure..." She paused to join him in laughing. "How about I give you a call or text when I'm leaving the office? Then I'll see you when you get there. I have a stock of wine...or beer, whatever you think might go best."

He pulled lightly on his erection, feeling a bit pervy doing so while she was unaware on the other end of the line, but just appreciating the contact. "I have a good idea of what you have there from my scouting the other day, when I cooked the thank you meal for you. You have a nice kitchen. I loved working in it. A bit more complete than Trev's." He huffed out a laugh, hoping he didn't sound as breathless to her as he did to his own ears. By all rights, he should let her get back to work then get himself off in the shower, but he hated to have the conversation end.

"It's true, neither one of us is nearly as handy in the kitchen as you are, so it's mostly a place to keep snacks and breakfast stuff. And coffee, of course, for us non-heathens who still drink it."

"Amen," he joked back. "I was shocked that he'd given it up." He licked his palm to give him a bit of glide. Really not wanting to talk about his brother while he was doing this, he steered them in another direction. "Well, for a woman who thinks of it as place to keep snacks, you definitely have about everything you'd need if you ever did want to do some cooking."

"I have my friend Rhon to thank for that. Restaurateurs always have it in their head that everyone loves the process as much as they do. And with the amount of time Rhonnie spends in my kitchen... Well, things just started showing up."

A surprising burst of jealousy hit him and he stopped the movement of his hand. *Who's Ron?* "Well, be sure to thank him for me," he tried to keep his tone casual and not accusatory, but he feared he sounded like a possessive ass.

"Her. That's right, I keep forgetting you haven't met her yet." She paused. "I guess you've only been here about a week—it seems like longer."

"Is that a good thing or a bad thing?" The question in his head left his mouth before he could prevent it.

"Oh, a very good thing. You're... I just really get along with you. It's nice."

Nice? Uh-oh. That was the kiss of death. He laughed at his wayward thoughts. "Well, I feel the same way about you." *Although I wouldn't use the word nice.* "Which is why I wanted to spend some time with you tonight." And that was the honest truth. Sexual attraction firmly aside—where it should be, by all rights, since she was taken—he felt very comfortable and in tune with Erica. She was a pleasure to be around.

Oh yes, a definitely pleasure...

He gripped his cock again, lightly massaging it, the sound of her voice adding to the enjoyable sensations.

"I'm so glad you called. I'd better get back to it. But I'll be in touch later on and see you soon." The smile was back in her voice. He loved that he could tell her moods so easily.

"Bye, Erica."

"Bye." The call disconnected and he laid the phone on the dresser before quickly crossing to the bathroom.

He started the water in the shower and when it had warmed, he stepped in and did a quick rinse. There was no debate needed—before anything else, he squeezed out a dollop of conditioner into his palm then stepped slightly out of the spray and slicked his semi-erection.

It didn't take much to coax it to a full stand. Colin began an easy rhythm as he closed his eyes. His mind went straight to Erica and her voice, her creamy skin and beautiful pale pink nipples…the way her mouth had been so warm and soft around his cock…and the incredible way she'd welcomed him into her body. No awkwardness, they'd moved together like they'd been partnered for years, in perfect sync.

He lingered on that memory of surging into her with her beautiful eyes focused intently on him, watching as he came…

Breathing hard, he threw his free hand up to brace himself on the wall as he jetted his cum onto the floor of the shower. He took a minute to recover and during that time, Erica's smiling face lingered in his mind.

* * * *

"Hi!" Erica opened the door wide for him. "Let me take that."

"Actually take this bag instead." Colin held out a reusable shopping bag to her and kept his firm hold on the warm, foil-covered casserole dish containing the enchiladas.

She accepted the bag and stood to the side to let Colin in then closed the door and trailed him into the kitchen. "Oh my God, whatever that is, it smells fantastic. My mouth is watering."

Colin grinned then impulsively turned and leaned to kiss her cheek before he walked over to set the dish on the stovetop. "Green chicken enchiladas. They're done—I just need to melt a bit of pepper jack on top. I wasn't sure if you had sour cream or other fixings, so I brought them along." He nodded towards the bag she still held.

"You're amazing. You're going to spoil me." She gave him a warm smile then began to unpack the contents of the bag. She paused before she lifted the small chili pepper plant out. "Is this for me?" she asked, examining it with delight. "It's so sweet. Are those edible?"

The plant had been an impulse buy for him. He'd gravitated towards the floral section when he'd gone shopping earlier, but he wasn't sure whether it was too romantic to bring a bouquet. So when he'd spotted the little pepper plants with the bright orange fruits hanging from them, he'd decided to keep to the Mexican theme. "Yes, I imagine they are, though they're kind of pretty just as décor."

"Oh definitely. I know just the place for you," she crooned to the plant and carried it over to the sink, above which was a kitchen window of the type made exactly for housing plants to maximize sun. It was exactly where Colin had pictured it going when he'd chosen it. She moved a few things around and gave it a place of honour then stepped back and admired it with a pleased expression.

"Thank you so much. I love it." She threw her arms around Colin and pressed against him for a tight hug. His eyes closed and he held her to him for several seconds, inhaling her already recognizable scent, before he reluctantly released her.

She stepped back with a hint of awareness in her eyes and her lips parted. Then she closed her mouth and turned away, breaking the spell. "So what can I do to help?"

Colin shook his head at himself and turned on the broiler. "Do you want to eat inside or out? Hmm, I guess it's getting a bit dark out there…"

"Why don't we eat inside, but maybe we can go sit outside and enjoy the evening afterwards?"

"Okay, that sounds good." He opened the pepper jack, which he'd bought pre-shredded to help minimise the prep, mindful of his earlier wish to not make a mess in her house, though he fully planned to do the few dishes too. After sprinkling the pan with cheese, he popped it under the heat to melt and meanwhile opened the sour cream and pico de gallo. "We'll keep this simple rather than dirty more dishes." He got out two spoons and plopped one each into the containers.

"Perfect." Erica grinned. "Believe it or not, I don't mind casual dining." She lowered his voice conspiratorially. "I even eat out of the carton sometimes."

They shared a laugh, Colin loving the image of the usually put-together Erica hunkered over a take-out container with a fork.

"So—do you have a plan for what to drink? I can get something out."

"Actually, I was just thinking we'd have a couple of those Dos Equis Ambers I saw in your beverage cooler. I brought some sliced limes."

"Oh, that's what the limes are for. I thought they were a garnish." She made a silly face. "Because I'm all about the accessories, of course." Erica walked over to the under counter glass-front fridge, opened it and pulled out two bottles of beer. Then to his surprise, she did something under the counter's edge to open them and neatly caught the tops in her hand.

He walked over to take a look at the mounted bottle opener then took the two open bottles from her. "Wow, that's handy. Very clever. More of Rhonnie's work?"

"Yes." Erica nodded ruefully. "I bought this place new and they were still finishing it, so she took over the kitchen plans and had them include this small fridge and the wine fridge in the pantry. And the window box. And the extra oven. And the bottle opener." She waved her hand around the room as Colin laughed.

He took slivers of lime and popped them into the bottles. "Cheers," he toasted and they clinked bottles. After a quick drink, he set his down then pulled the enchiladas from the oven. He set them on the stovetop and turned the broiler off. "Perfect timing. Do you want to grab some plates?"

Erica set two plates out then stood back and watched as Colin plated their helpings and garnished them with fresh cilantro, sour cream and the pico de gallo. "See? I did plan a garnish, just not the lime."

He carried the plate to the table and followed her lead as she set her bottle on the placemat at the head of the table, then put his next to hers in the same place he'd sat the other night.

It struck him how effortless it was to be with Erica. The camaraderie they shared was true and easy. He tried to thrust away the wishes he knew had no place in their lives and just enjoy his time with her.

They ate their meal, both of them going back for second helpings, and talked about various topics. The conversation never really lagged, though they didn't fill every single moment with chatter, sometimes content to simply enjoy the food and company.

After they'd cleared the kitchen—together, in spite of Colin's protests that she should sit and relax—they made cups of coffee and moved to the balcony. In addition to the chairs and table set, there was a loveseat glider, and it was there that Erica sat. Colin started to move towards a chair, but Erica beckoned him over, patting the seat next to her.

"Come try this out. It's really smooth and comfortable."

Colin changed direction and set down their coffees on the low table in front of the seat, then sat next to Erica. His weight set the glider in motion. "Wow. Doesn't take much to get it going, does it?"

"No, which is fine. I like rocking. It's very soothing to me." She sort of wriggled down into the cushion and lifted her feet to tuck them to the side up on the seat, angling herself in Colin's direction.

The moment just seemed to call out for him to hold her and he raised his arm along the back. She instantly settled in against him, and Colin wondered with a touch of bitterness whether this was something she did often with Trevor and if Colin was being used a substitute while he was gone. Immediately he tried to banish the thought, but he must have communicated his turmoil through tension in his body, because Erica lifted her head.

"I'm sorry, is this uncomfortable for you?"

"No, it's fine." He tried to relax.

She regarded him closely and began to sit up. "You seem tense."

Colin hugged her back to him with his arm, sorry that he'd let his petty thoughts ruin her enjoyment of the evening. "Really, it's okay. I just had one random thought, but I'm perfectly comfortable like this. I could sit here this way all night, actually."

She relaxed against him once again and let out a contented sigh. "Good. I love to sit outside and drink in the peace and quiet of this time of day. I hardly ever get to do it with company, though, and there's something about sharing the moment with someone else that's hard to replicate alone."

Colin debated for about two seconds before he asked the obvious question. "What about Trevor? You must do this with him, right?"

Erica let out a very unladylike snort. "Trevor?" She shook her head against his shoulder. "That would be like expecting a puppy to be still. You should know how he is. The only time he's not in motion is when he's asleep. It can get a bit—" She cut herself off abruptly and reached for her coffee.

He lifted his hold enough to allow her to reach the right angle to drink easily then smoothed his hand along her arm as she set her mug down and he accepted her back against him. What she'd said was true, now that he thought about it. Trevor seemed to be a bit of a wrong choice for a boyfriend for someone who seemed to relish quiet, companionable moments. He appreciated for Trevor's sake that she'd caught herself complaining about him and stopped, so while he really wanted to delve into it a bit more, he knew it was really none of his business and he let it go.

They rocked and sipped their coffees mostly in silence, with the occasional observation about the sunset and fading shadows playing across their view. Erica's weight seemed to gradually increase until Colin felt certain she'd fallen asleep, though he couldn't see her eyes to check. She was practically lying on him—her head had moved from his shoulder to his chest and when he put his other arm around her to embrace her, she reflexively snuggled against him in her sleep, breathing deeply.

It was the definition of bittersweet.

I am falling hard.

He swallowed and pressed his lips together.

What the hell am I going to do?

Chapter Eight

Erica dropped her robe before appreciative eyes that boldly roamed over her exposed body. Walking slowly towards the bed, she made sure to put a bit of extra seductive movement in her walk for her audience.

"Coffee?" she offered, stopping short of the bed.

He shook his head, watching her intently.

"Tea?" she teased, running her hands up her sides to cup her breasts and offer them forward.

A sexy smile and another shake of the head.

"Me?"

He answered her by surging forward and grasping her upper arms. She stood quiescent in his firm yet gentle grip as he leant forward to whisper in her ear.

"Hell yes." Then he dipped to take one of the proffered, peaked nipples in his warm mouth.

She moaned and let her head drop back, giving herself over to his attentions...

Colin...

Erica drifted in sleep, though she began to surface. Something didn't seem right. It was as though she was chilled and utterly warm and cosy at the same time.

She burrowed into the warmth and felt the movement of a hand on her arm. Frowning—wasn't Trevor out of town?—she managed to open her eyes then blinked as she realised she wasn't in bed, but outside on her balcony.

Gasping, she bolted upright, only to be soothed back into place with a shushing sound.

Colin…

She remembered now, swinging together and having coffee, then she must have conked out on him. Her cheeks heated up as she remembered her vivid power dream and she hoped she hadn't given any indication of what had gone on in her head. It was stupid to feel guilty about fantasising over Colin. After all, she had no control over her sleeping mind.

The whole situation was just a hard one to keep black and white. She knew first-hand exactly how Colin tasted, the feel of him exploring her body—with Trevor's full knowledge and blessing, no less. Why wouldn't her mind go there, especially when she'd been practically sleeping on top of him?

Grow up, she chided herself. *You're all adults.*

Maybe it was time to make Trevor talk about why he'd encouraged the scene to continue beyond the first unintentional mistake. She'd broached the subject one evening last week, but he'd just shrugged and changed the subject.

Colin shifted and she winced as she moved and prepared to stand. "Ohh… You must be stiff—I know I am. How long have we been out here?" It was now fully dark, so at least an hour. *Oops.*

He stretched his arms over his head then flexed his hand. "Not sure. And I'm not too bad, but my arm's asleep." He grinned at her as she blushed.

"Crap. Sorry about that. Hey, I can't help it if you're a really comfortable bed." She stood up and gathered their empty mugs, then walked towards the door to the living room. Erica could sense Colin moving behind her but what she saw in the reflection of the door made her laugh.

Amused, she spun around to watch him wincing while shaking his arm rapidly.

"Not funny! Pins and needles. Youch." He hissed in a breath then continued, "All because your big head cut off the blood flow to my arm."

She snickered and led the way inside. "My big head? It's not that big! And you could have woken me up."

He was down to rubbing his arm gently, his antics over. "Nah. You seemed so peaceful. I think you were even dreaming."

Erica cocked her head and she studied him closely. Was that a slightly knowing look? Or was she imagining things?

"I was," she admitted. "I've been kind of short of sleep lately."

Instantly his expression changed to concern. "Are you okay?"

Erica didn't answer right away, not sure how to skirt the real issue behind her lack of sleep—her quandary over Trevor and motherhood and now her growing attraction to Colin himself.

She must have left it too long, or maybe something in her expression betrayed her, because he crossed to her in two strides and took her by the upper arms then leaned in. It was so reminiscent of her dream that her breath caught.

Instead of whispering in her ear, though, he pulled her into a brief hug then set her away from him. "I just want you to know that I'm a good listener and I'm here for you. Even if what's troubling you is...close to home." He squeezed her arms again then took the mugs from her hands and went into the kitchen.

She suspected that he was alluding to Trevor, but she wondered if Colin could tell that part of what was keeping her up at night was him.

Close to home indeed.

Echoing the word *home* conjured up a strong image in her head of an evening spent much like this one...only the romantic scene on the balcony came after they'd tucked in a little one together and quietly left the room...

Oh for fuck's sake, Erica. You're hormonal enough.

It was especially cruel of her brain to have conjured that image now since she'd started her cycle the night before. As always, the reality of that time of the month seemed to mock her. *Another egg wasted. Tick tock.*

Feeling blue, she tried desperately to check her expression before Colin came back in. She only partially succeeded and could tell that he remained worried about her.

"I'll be fine, just need a good night's sleep."

Colin looked at her steadily. "I'm not sure whether to excuse myself so you can get started, or offer to stay since you obviously felt restful with me nearby."

Her mouth opened then closed as she considered that. It wasn't anything she would have thought of herself, but now her mind seized upon the idea of having him close.

"I'll stay if you want me to. Actually, I don't even have to stay all night, just until you conk off."

"No," she protested. "You'd better not run off in the middle of the night. You need your sleep too." She thought about what she'd just said. Evidently she'd just told him to stay. Suddenly becoming aware of how weary she was, she shrugged at an attempt at nonchalance. "Up to you, though."

Colin grinned slowly, his face lighting up as he nodded. "Fair enough. If that's up to me, then it's up to you where I sleep."

The smile that had formed in automatic response to his dropped. She hadn't really considered him sleeping *with* her, just staying in Trevor's room. Strangely enough, Trevor hadn't slept in her bed the few nights he'd been there before his trip. She hadn't thought much of it at the time, figuring he was banking sleep before his travels. But it puzzled her now.

Shaking that thought away for another time, Erica focused on the brother in front of her and boldly admitted, "I'd love if you slept with me. But," she warned, "no funny business."

"I wouldn't *dream* of it," he answered innocently.

Erica narrowed her eyes suspiciously at Colin and he smiled, chuckling inwardly. She must have been having a helluva dream while she'd been cozied up next to him outside. A couple of breathy sighs and a moan had slipped from her.

It had been arousing as hell to imagine that she was having a hot dream while he held her. He'd been enjoying the feel of her against him, even with his arm falling asleep, but once he'd figured out where her sleeping mind had gone, he'd held utterly still, trying not to disturb her.

Then, right before she'd awakened, she'd murmured his name—*Colin*...

His breath had caught and his insides had seized. He'd stiffened in surprise at what seemed to be a vocalization to a dream lover—to him—and she'd probably subconsciously felt his movement, because she woke up almost immediately.

Now he had another opportunity to hold her as she slept and he wasn't about to waste it. He knew that nothing would happen between them, that it would be as platonic as he could keep it. She seemed to be troubled greatly by something, and he just hoped it wasn't what had happened between them.

They went to start getting ready for bed, Erica in her bedroom and Colin in Trevor's room. The bed was mussed and it looked lived in, which surprised Colin. He knew Trevor had moved his belongings into the guest room, but he'd thought that was just to avoid Erica having to rearrange things so quickly.

But it looked to him like Trevor was more of a roommate to her than a live-in lover and boyfriend. Were they having problems? Was that what was on her mind? If that were the case, it wouldn't surprise him if she didn't confide in him. After all, Trevor and Colin had a close relationship, so she might want to keep anything to do with him to herself.

He did a quick rinse off in the shower then pulled on the silk sleep pants he'd bought Trevor. He had several pairs just like them, but he might keep these after today in retaliation for the sweats incident. That had him chuckling as he approached Erica's door. He stopped on the threshold.

"Are you ready for me?" he called. Well, that had come out a bit suggestive, damn it.

"Come on in," she invited from someplace across the room out of sight.

He walked in and admired her décor. The room was earth tones from light to dark, with small accents of black and sunshiny yellow. Very striking. "I love your colours in here."

"Thanks." Erica walked out of a door that must have been to a walk-in closet, since he could see the bathroom. She had her hair up in a messy bun and was wearing an oversized Teva T-shirt and blue plaid pyjama pants—obviously not dressed to seduce. That made it a bit easier.

He took his cue from her and climbed in on the other side of the bed once she'd got in. The king-sized bed ensured that they wouldn't need to touch—unless they intended to.

Colin finally said something he'd been wanting to say for a week now. "Thank you for that night. You have no idea what it meant to me."

He sensed Erica turn her head to look at him. Before she could speak, he continued, "Can I ask you a personal question?" Colin wanted to set his mind at ease.

"Sure." She turned over on her side to face him across the pillows.

He did the same. "Are you really okay with what happened that first night? I'd hate to think that that's what's keeping you up at night."

Her expression didn't change. "I had a feeling you might ask that. That's not what I'm…working through right now. It was…" She paused. "Well, I'm not sure how to describe it that won't come across wrong."

"Try," he urged. He wasn't about to be shy when for some reason her opinion mattered deeply to him.

She looked down at his chest then over at the wall, as though she couldn't quite meet his gaze.

Colin reached out and settled his hand undemanding atop hers but remained quiet. She would either answer or she wouldn't. He didn't want to push things.

"Keeping in mind that I'm dating your brother..." she began, then stopped. "Obviously." She huffed out a breath. "Queen Obvious. I swear, you wouldn't know that I make my living putting cohesive sentences together and improvising."

He laughed. She was so funny when she got irritated with herself.

"Okay—that night. It was great. Hot, sexy, fun...just amazing really. And I don't have any regrets, per se."

Wow, that was way more than he'd expected. But... "Per se? So you do feel something less than positive about it."

She quirked her lips. "Not really, other than the fact that experiencing that with someone other than the person I'm committed to doesn't sit easy on my conscience."

His eyebrows rose. "He was the one who instigated things. Has he given you reason to think he's upset about it?" Because Colin certainly hadn't got that impression from his brother. They really hadn't discussed it, and that fact really said everything right there. It was a non-issue.

"No, not at all. It's *me* that bothers me, if you get what I mean. The fact that he even came up with the idea is telling, I guess. But for me... Well, I suppose it just proved to me that—" She closed her eyes. "I really shouldn't be discussing this with you. Why am I telling you this? I should be talking to Trevor."

Colin knew that the conversation was better tabled, either temporarily or permanently. "No worries," he reassured her. "I just selfishly wanted to make sure you weren't upset with me for my part in things."

Erica smiled at him, her tension slowly dissipating. "You're about the least selfish person I know. And I'm not upset with you. Quite the opposite."

They lay there for a few minutes, quietly taking each other in. Erica's eyelids began to look heavy and Colin was glad to see that she seemed to be heading towards a restful night.

"Is it selfish of me if I wish you could hold me again?" she murmured.

"Quite the opposite," he returned and without hesitation he raised his arm invitingly. She moved towards him then flipped over to face away from him as he brought her back against him, her ass wriggling for just a moment against his soft cock before she found a comfortable position.

It wanted to stir, but he fought the sensation, not wanting to break the peace of the moment. He realised with amusement that it was the first time in over a year that he wished his cock *wouldn't* get hard.

As his mind raced and his senses were filled with Erica, he was glad she would finally have a good night's sleep.

But it didn't look good for it being a restful one for him.

Chapter Nine

"So exactly how is it that you went to go break up with him, and ended up having him move in?"

It was the first time she'd managed to get together with Rhonnie since the night she'd sat here in her restaurant and planned to break things off. Erica gave an unladylike snort and pressed her lips together, glaring at her friend as she put into voice the very question Erica'd been asking herself for weeks now.

How? she wanted to respond. *Because I was so caught off guard by the afterglow of amazing sex while fucking his twin brother that when he asked if he could move in with me so Colin could use his condo, I said, "Sure. That'd be great."*

Apparently coming that hard affected her brain.

"He wanted to let his brother stay in the condo while he looked for a place to live now that he's back stateside," she said instead, dancing around the real question. "And we were sleeping together at one place or another almost every night anyway…"

Rhonnie glared right back. "Don't think that I don't realise that you just totally avoided the question. Not becoming. You know that it's me you're talking to, right? Someone who knows you inside and out?" She rolled her eyes and gave a put-upon sigh. "Okay, so if you're not going to talk about that, how about the artificial insemination. Have you chosen a donor yet?"

Erica winced. She hadn't really thought about it since 'the night'. "No, not yet."

"But you've picked a sperm bank?"

"Uh...no."

"Have you even talked to your fertility specialist? Let me guess. No. Erica..." Rhon took her hand. "Are you putting this off because of Trevor and the whole living together thing you got talked into? Or because you're not ready? Because last I heard, you *were* ready."

Erica knew that she *had* been, but with the advent of Colin into her life and the crazy dueling feelings she was having between the two men, finding the conviction to move forward with her plans had taken a back seat. She kept telling herself that it was good to feel one hundred per cent certain before she went any further with her plans to become a single mother. Realistically, though, was anyone ever completely sure about a major life change?

"I am. I just..." Erica sighed. "I don't know. Maybe I'm not ready. I thought I was until..."

"Until what?"

Until I figured out how fickle I can be after meeting Colin. Which begged the question, if she were that indecisive about the men in her life, what made her think that her mind was clear on what she should do to have a child?

When it came right down to it, what was holding her back was probably the utterly unrealistic hope that somehow her dreams would come to fruition—no pun intended—without having to go the clinical route. *Ain't gonna happen.* The man in her life was sometimes little more than a kid himself and very against ever having children.

"I have to pee." Rhonnie levered her increasing girth up from the table. "So you get a reprieve for now. Just think about it," she tossed back over her shoulder as she swayed towards the bathroom.

Erica had no problems doing just that. Thinking about it was *all* she'd been doing since that night. She had spent a great deal of time with both brothers in the past few weeks and had learnt an uncomfortable truth about herself. While she still loved Trevor, it was Colin to whom she was drawn, with a pull that went well beyond what she could remember from the beginning of her relationship with Trevor. And his somewhat toned down, mature personality meshed more fully with hers and her interests. Where Trevor was always on the go and extremely high energy, Colin enjoyed the same quiet pursuits she craved during her downtime. Her job was demanding enough—on her time off, she wanted to relax, both physically and mentally.

Dealing with her unexpected attraction to Colin had pulled her focus somewhat from her fertility. It had also spiked a longing for the kind of passionate and companionable relationship she could see as possible with Colin. Which made her leery about taking action on getting inseminated—because with that longing came the wishful hope she could have the whole package…a partner and fellow parent, in one man.

That man obviously wasn't Trevor.

And unfortunately, even if they somehow got around her being with his brother, it couldn't be Colin either. She had heard the horrific details about his accident from Colin, and privately mourned with him the loss of his fertility, feeling empathy for him, especially at such a young age. At least she still had options. His injury had been effectively a brutal vasectomy. With side effects.

Erica flushed as she recalled the discomfiting and bizarre thank you Colin had offered for their intimate encounter. She couldn't imagine what it must have been like to experience impotence for such a long period as a twenty-six-year-old.

And you *turned him on to the point where he got past it. Go you.*

She admired how he appeared to have retained his confidence and had a really great attitude about moving forward. But she couldn't help but feel a twist of jealousy at the thought of Colin sleeping with another woman, probably someone gorgeous and young and svelte, like him.

Pretty two-faced of you to begrudge him that, or did you forget you're dating someone else?

Kind of hard to forget, now that Trevor was sharing her home. But in a way, it had been a good experiment. She knew for certain now that she and Trevor wouldn't work out long-term. But the impetus to break it off still eluded her, even though she got a strong vibe that he wouldn't be heartbroken.

What I need is a sign. A nudge. Something. Any*thing.*

Frustrated at her lack of decisiveness and angst, she banged her head on the table.

"Hey, hey, don't do that."

The resonant voice hit her libido just as the strong arm pulling her back into a semi-hug made her vibrate with need. "Colin."

"You can tell us apart without even looking. Very impressive." His breath teased in her ear, and she closed her eyes for a moment, swaying towards him, accepting his light kiss on her lips. It clung for a shade too long to be considered strictly platonic, and her eyes popped open as he withdrew. Just a tease, and much less than she wanted, but all she could take under the circumstances.

She watched as he slid into the chair next to her and scooted it close to her. He took her hand, stroking his thumb lightly over the back of hers. Colin was extremely tactile and affectionate, too, much more so than his brother. And she ate it up. Needed it.

Craved it.

Quit with the comparisons!

"Aww, you guys are cute." Rhon retook her seat. "Hey, Trevor."

Erica opened her mouth with a rebuttal, but Colin answered first with a mischievous smile. "Hi there. Are you lovely ladies having a nice lunch?"

He looked at Erica as though daring her to set the record straight, and she found herself playing along, enjoying the joke. She'd tell Rhonnie his real identity any minute now... "Oh yes, and it's getting better every second," she flirted back.

Rhonnie got a determined glint in her eye. "So, we were just talking about the two of you moving in together."

"Oh?" Colin questioned, giving Erica a sidelong glance. She refused to look in his direction, instead lifting her eyebrows in warning at Rhonnie.

"Yep. She was just saying it was kind of temporary until your brother—Colin, right?—finds his own place. How's the search going for him? You must be anxious to get back into your own home."

"Rhon," Erica warned under her breath, but her friend ignored her, and now Colin was picking up the gauntlet.

"Oh, he's narrowing it down, but it might be a little while. We're actually both looking at houses right now. We might just end up buying a bigger place together."

That was news to Erica. "Really?" she blurted, then could have kicked herself when they both turned to look at her. "I mean, *we* haven't really talked about that." Inwardly, she wondered why Trevor hadn't even mentioned it to her. Was he feeling their relationship was nearing the end as well? Or was she just putting a nefarious spin on his lack of communication on the topic when he probably just forgot to bring it up?

And then there was the fact that Colin hadn't said anything either.

"Well, we're both making much better money now than we did when he bought this place. If we pool our equity and income, we can expand our search to include some really nice places right on the beach."

"Wait a minute. When '*he*' bought the place? Don't you mean, when *you* bought it?" Rhonnie's eyes narrowed, and Erica watched, amused, as Colin flushed at the mistake.

"Damn. See, you guys got me talking. I was never the one who could pull a switch off. Trev's much better at it. He has me down pat."

Rhonnie's eyes were huge as she looked back and forth between Erica and Colin, with a pointed glance at their linked hands. "Okaaay. So...nice to meet you, *Colin*."

"You too. You must be the infamous Rhonnie. Thanks for all you did for her kitchen, by the way."

Rhonnie blinked, still staring at Colin, trying to keep up. "You're welcome. Do you cook then?" She shook her head abruptly and spun towards Erica. "And you! You didn't mention they were twins — why?"

"Well, it goes back to their mother. Remember that day we met Trevor and he said he and his brother were fathered by a donor?" Rhonnie nodded and Erica continued, "That's just a way that their mom started from the get-go to keep them from becoming labelled as 'the twins' or not thought of as individuals."

Rhonnie appeared thoughtful and she looked back at Colin. "Well, I can understand that, especially if you've always looked this much alike. Though, now that I look at you, you're a bit...less muscular than Trevor."

"Yes, yes — the über-muscles. Erica has already made that clear." He smiled despite his words to show that he wasn't really upset at the comparison.

"Still, come on — regardless of what they refer to themselves as, them being identical twins is worth a mention to your best friend at least. I mean, you'd think it would have come up sometime in the past several months."

Erica cleared her throat. "Well, I only just found out myself when I...met Colin a few weeks ago." Oh God, she'd almost said *slept with*. She just about burst out laughing at the expression that would have been on Rhonnie's face at that kind of slip.

Colin was just sitting back and enjoying the debate, still toying with Erica's hand. Just then, Rhonnie brought it into the equation.

"That's another thing," she accused. "The gig is up, so why are you still playing kissy-face with the whole holding hands bit?"

"He's just affectionate that way," Erica explained airily, loving the chance to have her super-sharp friend guessing at what the hell was going on.

"I am," Colin dutifully agreed.

"Affectionate. Huh."

"Needy?" Erica ventured. "Clingy?"

Colin frowned. "Clingy makes me sound like I need a dryer sheet."

Erica giggled, unable to keep up the unaffected pose. "But you didn't debate needy. Case closed." She smiled up at Colin and he brushed her hair back at the temple with his free hand.

Rhonnie had been watching them like a spectator at a tennis match, her brow creased. "Oh my God. Am I seeing what I think I'm seeing?" she asked herself aloud.

Erica sobered abruptly at the probing look Rhonnie was giving her and disengaged her hand from Colin's as unobtrusively as possible.

Rhonnie's gaze flicked to Colin then back. She sighed, used her napkin then set it on the table. "I can see I'm not going to get anything useful out of you two jokers, so I'm going to work."

Erica glanced at her iPhone, which she'd silenced before lunch, and cringed when she saw the time and how many messages had piled up. "Guess I'm off, too."

"I'll walk you," Colin offered to Erica, while assisting Rhonnie to her feet.

"Thanks," the women chorused, then rolled their eyes in tandem. "Call you tomorrow," Erica added as Rhonnie slowly made her way through the tables.

"You'd better," she was told, with a smile to soften the warning in her eyes that told Erica she would be in for a grilling.

She strolled with Colin at her side, his hand hovering on her lower back. The heat radiated from the simple point of contact throughout her body, making her utterly aware of his proximity. Remembering how that hand had felt on her body, she felt her nipples pucker, making her glad she had a jacket on over her blouse. As it was, she had to shrug to adjust the press of her bra against the taut peaks.

They chatted about neutral topics for most of the four-block walk, the conversation only turning personal when they reached the broadcast company's building and Erica indicated her entrance.

Colin stepped in front of her before she could move in that direction. "Are you upset to hear that Trevor is definitely planning for this to be temporary? Or relieved?"

Erica couldn't mask her shock. "You don't beat around the bush, do you?"

Colin simply waited for a response, and the palpable feel of him lingering well inside her personal space was making it hard to think. Her lips parted of their own accord as she willed his to descend, to take the choice away from her and fulfil her growing need for him. But even though his gaze dropped to caress her mouth, Colin didn't make a move to touch her.

Frustrated and a bit horrified with her lack of control, she took a step back. "I'm not upset," she finally answered. "But I can't say I'm relieved either. It's…fine. I like Trevor, and he's easy to live with." She wasn't about to say that she and Trevor hadn't had sex since…well, since the time with Colin.

Colin met her gaze steadily. "Erica, I'm hearing 'fine' and 'like' and 'easy' and those are hardly the descriptors I'd expect from someone in a serious relationship. Are you in love with him?"

Erica looked away, unable to maintain eye contact. "I shouldn't be having this conversation with you."

"I'm exactly who you should be talking about this with," he countered, and she snapped her eyes up to meet his, drawn by the intensity and demand in his voice. "And you know why, don't you, Erica? Now tell me — are you in love with my brother?"

Chapter Ten

Colin knew he was pushing, but he couldn't stop himself. He had to know how she felt, once and for all. If she truly did love Trevor, he would back off, even help them to work together as a couple if possible. But during this past month of getting to know her and being with her, he'd realised she was the one he'd been searching for, the one he wanted in the forever kind of way.

Now, if he could just get Erica and Trevor to admit they weren't working out.

In a response he didn't expect, hadn't foreseen in all the different ways he'd envisioned when mentally rehearsing this moment, she turned the tables on him. "Are you trying to tell me you want me to love you instead?"

Wow. What a woman, he admired, even as he squirmed at being under the microscope, laid out for her dissection. She'd cut to the heart of the matter. It was true. What else could he do, but admit it? "Yes."

Her brow puckered in the way he'd become familiar with. "We've only known each other for a month. Less than that, even. You don't know the first thing about me, about what's important to me."

Relieved at finally getting the chance to make his case, he pressed on. "It's been plenty of time for me to know that we fit in every way possible. We enjoy many of the same things, we have this amazing chemistry between us." He pulled her snugly against him, uncaring of the people around them and the semi-erection now pressed against her stomach. "And I like you." He looked steadily into her eyes as he confessed, "I'm growing to love you."

"Colin..." Erica shook her head, and tried to pull out of his embrace. He reluctantly let her go, but stayed close.

"If you're in love with Trev, I'll be happy for you. Truly. But if you aren't, I want you to give us a chance." Colin then forced himself to wait, heart hammering in his chest. It was a lot to lay out all at once. But when he'd seen her today, it had hit him like a semi—he couldn't suppress his feelings for her for another minute.

She shook her head once more. "I'm sorry, Colin. I just can't."

"Do you love him?" he demanded uneasily, feeling control of the moment slipping away.

The sad look on her face was breaking his heart. "No," she whispered.

Hope leapt again. "Then why not? Just give us a chance," he repeated. "I'll wait for you to talk to Trev. I'll even do it for you...with you...whatever you like."

He watched as her temper flared, her eyes snapping with anger. Or was it fear? "It's not about Trevor. Okay? It's you—you just can't give me what I'm looking for, and I know what I need to be happy. It would never work between us."

Feeling that blow almost physically, as though he'd taken a direct hit to his chest, he took a step back, then another. He nodded brusquely, needing to preserve some of his pride. "Point taken. My mistake."

He turned away, catching out of the corner of his eye her hand as it rose as if to halt his flight. It never made contact, and he walked away, the silence of her lack of reply tolling his ears.

* * * *

"You're *what*?" Trevor's shock was written across his face, and it almost immediately morphed into hurt and anger.

Colin repeated the words stoically. "I'm going back to Asia for another year."

"What the hell? You just got back a month ago, and you said you were never leaving the States again. You have plenty of jobs lined up—so many you're turning them down." Trevor raked a hand through his hair, then unexpectedly reached out and pushed Colin in frustration, knocking him back a step. "No! You can't go."

He pressed his lips together. His brother's reaction, while not unexpected, wasn't exactly making it any easier to think about leaving. "There's nothing holding me here. Might as well make some coin."

"What about *me*?" Trevor practically shouted, shoving him again, and Colin balled up his fists to keep from shoving back. "And what about Erica?"

Colin inhaled sharply, his heart pounding. "What *about* Erica? What does she have to do with anything?"

Trevor shook his head. "You've always been a horrible liar, Col." He started pacing. "Everything. She has everything to do with this. Why you think you should go, *and* why you should stay." He whirled towards Colin and pointed a finger at him. "Don't think I've missed what's been growing between you. I might not be the smart one, but I'm not stupid." Trevor pinned Colin with his eyes, daring him to try lying.

All of the guilt he'd been holding in about his feelings for Erica swamped him at once. It came out as anger. "You have a lot of nerve, implying anything. Erica would never cheat on you, and I would never do that to you either."

Trevor snorted. "I know that. Jesus. You two are saints. I swear it took everything I had in me not to break up with her weeks ago and give you guys the green light."

"What?" Colin froze and stared at Trevor, who continued talking with barely a pause.

"But it was too soon—you had to cement the connection. Oh, the vibes were there" —he waved his hand in the air—"but you needed to get to know each other with the pressure off first."

Colin's mind whirled in confusion. "What? What the hell are you talking about?" His eyes narrowed on his brother as an awful suspicion occurred to him. "Did you set up that first night somehow? Getting us in bed together?"

"Man, I wish, but no. That was pure karma. But it came to me first while I was watching you together that night, then over the weeks since, watching the connection grow between you two. You're a much better match for her than me." Trevor shrugged, smiling ruefully. "Erica's great, and if I can't make her happy, I want her to have the best—which is you."

Colin sagged a bit, his mind spinning. All in all, he was relieved that his secret was now out in the open and he could talk about things with his brother, who was also his best friend. He looked closely at Trevor and couldn't sense a hint of sadness at losing Erica, whereas the same situation was flat out killing him. Frustration won out over his confusion.

"Tell that to her. She flat out rejected any thought of being with me. So it's a moot point either way."

"Tell me exactly what she said," Trevor countered.

Colin had no desire to relive that moment and he stayed silent.

"Seriously, do you want Erica or not? What did she say?"

He thought back over the confrontation on the street. "Well, I asked her to tell me whether she truly loved you or not." He glared at Trevor. "At the time, I had no idea you two were already over in your mind. That might've been good to know."

Trevor just cocked an eyebrow and waited.

"I finally got her to admit that she didn't love you." What a bizarre conversation. "And I as much as told her that I loved her and wanted her to give us a chance." He thought a moment, then added, "And I said that I'd wait for her to talk to you, or I would, or we could go together." He sighed. Then she'd broken his heart.

"And what did she say to that?"

He shrugged miserably. "Something like, it wasn't about you" — he pointed to Trev — "but it was me. That I can't give her what she's looking for and that it wouldn't work between us."

Trevor nodded somberly. "I can see how that would sound pretty bad. I'm sorry." He moved closer and put his hands on Colin's shoulders, looking him straight in the eye. "With me out of the picture, there's only one thing keeping you two apart in her mind. And I know how to fix it. Call your client. Tell them you're not going to China. Don't run away from this. Don't leave us."

Colin swallowed against the internal battle his brother's confidence engendered, competing with the sadness he'd been holding onto. It was as though a nest of demented butterflies were warring in his stomach. "Trev. I have to go. I can't be here, knowing she doesn't want to be with me."

His brother grasped the back of his neck and squeezed reassuringly. "Don't go. I promise I can make this happen. Trust me." Those familiar eyes willed him to believe, and despite his best efforts, Trevor's assurance kindled a flicker of hope in Colin. "Stay. And we'll get Erica for you. Guarantee it."

Colin wavered then he finally gave up all sense of self-preservation and reluctantly smiled. Trevor grinned back then pulled him into a back-pounding hug.

"Okay, I'm going to get us a couple of beers and you're going to tell me exactly why you're so convinced you can 'fix it'. *Capisce*?"

Colin headed into the kitchen without waiting for a response, needing a moment away from his brother's intense regard. He grabbed two bottles from the fridge then rummaged through drawers trying to find an opener. That, of course, made him think of Erica and her Rhonnie-approved kitchen. He sighed and gave up.

"Where the hell is a bottle opener?"

"Up on the corkboard."

"Of course," Colin muttered walking across the room to the cluttered board and finally spotted a lizard on a chain that evidently doubled as a bottle opener. He figured it out and opened the bottles, then slipped the chain around his neck in case they needed it later.

He found Trevor outside on the deck and handed him his beer.

"Nice accessory." Trev gestured with the bottle to the chain, then clinked tops with Colin as he sat.

Colin settled back and waited for Trevor to start explaining. Trevor knew what he wanted to hear and damned if he was going to beg for information. It was enough that he was putting his heart in his brother's hands.

"Remember the accident?" Trevor began.

Colin blinked. That hadn't exactly been the direction he'd expected the conversation to go. "Duh. Every day when I take a shower."

Trevor grimaced in apology, looking uncharacteristically serious. "I know. I mean, do you remember after, when I decided to pull my donations at the sperm bank?"

Oh. No wonder he looks like a kicked puppy. "Trev, I love you, but you seriously need to let go of the guilt on that. It was not your fault."

Trevor shrugged and Colin took that to mean that he was going to stubbornly continue to believe what he wanted to believe on that topic. "Yeah, well. My point is"—he leant forward—"you know the reason why I did that. And I think we're there."

Colin frowned for a moment then he suddenly got it. "Whoa. Wait a minute." He held his hands up in shock. "We're not even together, much less at the point where we'd talk about a family. It's not exactly like we're going to jump into familyhood anytime soon."

Trevor looked thoughtful. "Okay, let's table that for a minute. Did I ever tell you how I met Erica?"

Colin searched his memory. "I think you said you ran into her at a café and hit it off. Rhonnie's place probably?" he checked.

"Yep. But what got us talking was, I overheard Erica and Rhonnie talking about sperm donors." He laughed at the memory. "You should have heard what Erica had to say about the sort of guy who'd donate."

Colin chuckled. "And you jumped in to set the record straight."

"Well, yeah. Why wouldn't I?" Trevor spread his hands wide.

Colin had no answer for that one.

"Anyway, if I were you, the next question I'd have would be, why were they discussing sperm banks..." Trevor paused encouragingly.

"For Rhonnie?" Colin stated the obvious.

"Nope, she was already pregnant. For Erica."

Colin's jaw dropped. "Erica? Why...?" He tried to think. "I mean...she's never mentioned anything about it to me."

"Had a lot of personal conversations, have you?"

He cleared his throat. "One or two."

"Sure. Anyway, I know she really wants to have a baby, and she's not getting any younger. So she'd just about decided to go that route..."

Colin waited for Trevor to continue. When he didn't, he asked, "What happened?"

Trevor shrugged. "I'm not sure exactly. We started dating. She sounded me out once or twice about my thoughts on fatherhood but you know that's just not me. Which is why we're just not right for each other in the long run. But you..." He leaned in. "You've always known you wanted a family. Which is why what happened to you was…" He stopped and bowed his head. "A fucking crime. And that's why I took my donations off the market, so to speak, out of respect for your future partner."

They so rarely spoke seriously, it was surreal. Colin was honestly amazed to see this side of Trevor.

"Col, I've never seen you the way you are with Erica, and that's even with the brakes on because of our relationship. You're so happy you fucking glow. I'm pretty sure she's the one — your forever one."

"You can't just fast forward through things to a positive pregnancy test."

Trevor cocked an eyebrow but still wore a serious expression. "Do you know how old Erica is?"

"I have a feeling you're going to tell me."

"She's going to be forty-five soon."

Colin silently processed that. It was older than he'd thought — and well older than she looked and acted — but that didn't really matter to him.

However, if she was determined to have a baby, she must be constantly watching the clock, frantically trying to figure out a way to make it happen before it was too late, if it already wasn't.

Then she'd started dating a man with no desire for children. No wonder she didn't think things would work in the long run with Trevor. And as for him…

'…*you just can't give me what I'm looking for, and I know what I need to be happy.*'

"Let me ask you this," Trevor cut into the thoughts whirling in his head. "Do you love her?"

Colin nodded, not sure he could trust his voice.

"The forever kind." It was a statement, not a question but Colin nodded again. "If it's the real deal, you need to go for it. Because when you put yourself out there, right or wrong, she took the baby thing into consideration when she turned you away. But if that wasn't an issue…"

"If you were to father the baby…" Colin felt a sense of rising hope.

"Then it'd be a win win…win. You'd get the girl, she'd get her dream and I'd get…to sleep with her at least a few more times."

Colin's jaw dropped at his brother's lascivious look. He smacked his shoulder. "Are you kidding me? *That's* your motivation?" He wasn't sure how he felt about Trevor and Erica being together if he and Erica were to become serious, but if it was for a purpose…

It was a little hypocritical to be prissy about it after how intimate Trevor had already been with her.

"Okay, okay…fine. I would get to give you two the most precious gift of all and make you happy and complete, which would mean so much to me because I love you both."

There was silence between them for a moment.

"Wow. You said that with a straight face." Colin shook his head. Yes, definitely the most surreal conversation they'd ever had.

"Well, yeah, because I meant every word. Sheesh, you'd think I was shallow or something. I was baring my heart there." Trevor managed to look wounded then broke into laughter. "Seriously!"

"I know, Trev. I know." And he did. Trevor loved him like no one else on earth, beside their mom. If there was anything one brother could do for the other, they would.

Even something like getting their girlfriend or wife pregnant.

Or giving up a wonderful woman for the other one.

Best. Brother. Ever.

Chapter Eleven

Erica closed down her laptop and wearily pushed back from her kitchen counter. Trevor had just had dinner delivered and was unpacking the bags of Chinese when his phone rang. He tapped on his Bluetooth and answered.

"Hello? Oh, hey, Col."

She looked up then hastily back down. She hadn't seen Colin since the day before when they'd parted ways in front of her building.

When you threw his love back in his face…

Erica rubbed her suddenly stinging eyes. She hadn't realised how attached she was to Colin until they'd gone silent. The past twenty-hour hours or so had been the longest and bluest of her life.

"Well, shit. That's good, I guess. I'm going to be sorry to see you go, jerk, but at least I'll get my own condo back. So, are you going to be living in the same place when you go back to China?"

What? Her stomach thudded as it dropped. *Colin was going back to Asia?* Erica had thought he was done working overseas, that he had vowed never to go so far away from his family again. It had been hard being across the city from him for one day, much less half a world away for a year.

"Good thing we didn't end up putting a bid in on a place, but maybe next year… I know, I know… No, I'll be back in town on Saturday… Sure, I can give you a ride."

Saturday? Oh God. So soon.

What's the matter? You weren't going to get involved with him, remember?

Erica tried lecturing her soul about the reason for not going there, which just reminded her brain about the excruciating conversation when Colin had bared his heart to her.

And she'd sliced it up and delivered it back with a side of wasabi.

With her own heart as a garnish.

She'd had to grit her way through her denial of him, all the while wanting to throw herself into his arms, her heart soaring and aching at the same time to hear his pleading for a chance at her love. Her palms still bore the brunt of the encounter where her nails had broken the skin.

Trevor had evidently hung up and was looking at her with a curious expression on his face. She made an effort at controlling her expression, but knew she didn't manage to succeed.

"I think it's well past time that we had a talk, sweets." Trevor seemed unusually sombre. Maybe he was just sad about Colin leaving again? No—she knew this was going to be the talk where they made a big decision. "Come on," he beckoned her.

Oh, why did he have to choose now, when her reserves were so low? But she obediently followed him into the living room, and they sat together on the couch overlooking the city view.

Trevor linked his fingers together and looked her straight in the eye before he began. "We work well together, but we both know this isn't a grand romance. Right?" He paused as if to gauge her response, and she gave a nod, relieved that this didn't seem as though it was going to turn into a scene. She began to relax.

Then Trevor continued, "So there's no reason you and Colin can't make this thing between you work."

She stiffened in shock, giving an involuntary gasp. The sound of the blood rushing in her ears was the only warning she had before she began to fall apart. Never had she imagined that Trevor would sense her interest in Colin. "Colin isn't... I mean, we're not... We never—" She cut herself off and tried to gather her scattered wits as Trevor pulled her against his side.

"I know you 'never' and you never would as long as the two of us were together. Which is why I'm calling the couple part of us quits. But even though we won't be together that way anymore, I've got your back. Which is why you need to see Colin, and give him a chance."

Erica refused to meet his gaze or respond, her throat aching with the effort of holding her emotions in check. She was a strong, professional woman, damn it. She would not be reduced to a blubbering idiot by relationship problems.

"There's no reason you shouldn't be with him," Trevor said softly. "I know you *think* there is, but it's a moot point."

Startled, she found herself needing to argue back, even though she'd told herself to ignore, ignore, *ignore* anything to do with Colin. "Even if you think you know why, how can you say it's not a factor? It *is* a factor. It's not just a silly whim. This is something I've been wanting for a very long time, and—"

"And have you ever checked to see whether Colin would be okay with you using a donor to father a child you could raise together? Or adopt together? Have you ever given him the benefit of the doubt?" Trevor pinned her with a pointed look, his eyebrow raised.

She dropped her eyes guiltily. The answer, of course, was no.

"You didn't with me either. Oh, you were right in my case." He smirked. "I'm not now, nor will I ever be, ready to be a dad. I like my life just the way it is. But Colin? He's different. I know he wants to have kids. And I suspect that using a donor—which is incidentally his only option for having kids other than adoption now—would be just fine with him...

"Especially if the donor carried the exact same DNA," he concluded with a smug grin, and Erica's heart nearly stopped.

Could it really be that simple?

Her mouth worked, but she couldn't pull everything together to make a coherent sentence come out. Suddenly, the best of both worlds was laid in her lap. Did she dare reach out and grab hold?

A horrible thought flashed through her mind. "But he's leaving, moving to Asia! Oh, and he probably hates me after what I said to him."

"All that aside, just answer me one thing. Are you in love with him?"

The question was almost exactly the same one she'd heard from the other brother. But it wasn't *déjà vu* when it came to the answer that tumbled immediately out, straight from her soul.

"Yes."

"Then go to him."

Erica jumped to her feet, the mere suggestion enough to get her in motion. "Where?"

"In your bedroom."

She froze. The faint voice wasn't coming from Trevor. It came simultaneously from somewhere in the condo and from the Bluetooth. Trevor gave her a grin as he pulled it from his ear, then impatiently gestured to the hallway. "Go on. I'll leave you some dinner you two can warm up later. The 'delivery guy' made sure there was enough for all three of us." He winked.

Erica gave Trevor a quick, impulsive hug, and turned to find Colin hadn't waited for her to come to him, even though he could have. Even now, having apparently overheard everything, there was a trace of uncertainty in his eyes as he watched her approach, as if he expected to be rejected again.

The damn tears welled up again, and she catapulted across the room and into his arms. Feeling them close around her, she knew with certainty that she was home. Needing to give Colin the same reassurance, she stroked his face, marveling at the warmth in his brown eyes as he looked down at her with a faint smile.

"I do love you, and I think I'm *in love* with you too," she declared, wanting to show him she was willing to put herself out there as he did.

It was like she'd given him the moon, evidenced by the utterly relieved and happy smile he gave her right before he kissed the daylights out of her.

She poured herself into the kiss, nearly climbing him in her desire to get as close as humanly possible. She'd gone from pining from afar, to excising him from her life, to the fear of him moving an ocean away in such a short amount of time—all those emotions drove her need to be with him—now—and never let him go.

Colin cupped her ass and with a small hop, she was wrapped around him like a baby monkey, never pausing in her own exploration of his face, his back, his hair. They finally parted for breath and he mouthed his way down her neck. Abruptly, he spun around and braced her up against the wall. Caught between the immoveable structure and Colin's unyielding body, she rotated her pelvis as he settled in the perfect spot in the cradle of her thighs. His hard cock was a brand against her pussy and it ignited an urgent need to have him inside her as soon as possible.

"Bed," she gasped out as he ran a hand up under her shirt then inched it under the band of her bra to just brush her nipple.

She slowly opened her eyes—when had she closed them?—froze for a moment, then burst out laughing.

Trevor was sitting on the couch holding a plate of food and chopsticks, eating while watching them make out. "What?" he said around a mouthful of food. "He knew I was watching. Dinner and a show." He waved the chopsticks in their direction. "Carry on."

Colin smiled against her neck then gave her a gentle kiss on the same spot before straightening up and walking down the hall carrying Erica. She gave Trevor a smile and cheeky wave goodbye before he disappeared from view.

"Boo," he called after them. "Spoilsports!"

Colin carried her into her bedroom and kicked the door mostly closed behind him.

"Are you ever going to put me down?" she asked against his mouth.

"You're such a tiny thing," he murmured into her neck as he let her slide down his front, keeping full contact with her body as her breasts rubbed down his chest. He cupped her buttocks as he lowered her, grinding against her as her pussy glided across his hardened shaft. "I could hold you up like this for hours."

Oh my God. The visual that comment prompted of him nailing her to the wall — *sans* clothes this time — had her grabbing his neck and wildly seeking his mouth again. He smiled with delight dancing in his eyes and gave her another soul-searing kiss before firmly moving her away from him.

"Let's get undressed. I've been dying to get you naked again."

The thought of doing a striptease crossed her mind for a moment, then fled. She shed her clothing with alacrity and efficiency as Colin did the same. He finished first and stepped towards the bed, never once taking his admiring eyes from her. She undid her bra last and shrugged it from her shoulders. Her nipples perked immediately upon contact with the cool air and Colin's gaze. Erica walked over and sat on the edge of the bed, crooking her finger to coyly beckon him closer.

He stepped up, seemingly content to let her set the pace now. She stroked his rigid shaft, looking in wonder at its perfection contrasted against the scarring below, before bending to tentatively kiss the old injury. His intake of breath gave her even more incentive to make sure he was confident in her love for him. She wrapped her hand around the base of his cock as she licked him slowly around and across the head, feeling the slit with her tongue and tasting his tangy essence.

Growing impatient, she took him into her mouth partway, wrapping her lips over her teeth to bite down gently, testing his firmness, then loosening her jaw and using her tongue to soothe. She suckled strongly and he groaned, grasping her head and gently directing her in taking and releasing him as he fucked her mouth with shallow thrusts.

Erica felt so in tune with Colin. When she had made the difficult decision to turn his love away, she never could have dreamt she would have him back with her, on such a positive track to the future. She had wanted more than just a lasting connection, a relationship — she'd wanted a family, a man to be with, to share her love and life with.

Erica pushed Colin back a step so she could slide to her knees on the floor before him. She smiled wryly as he responded to the different angle with an increase in the pressure of the fingers tangled in her hair. She trailed her fingertips down the deep, muscular V arrowing from the bottom of his abdominals to the base of his cock. Her pussy ached with the void she increasingly felt, needing him to fill her, but she was so enjoying the feel of his cock on her tongue and stretching her lips.

Choices, choices.

She added a hand to his shaft, squeezing and pumping lightly in time with her suction, then cradling his sac, learning the weight and feel of his remaining ball, giving it gentle attention.

Colin couldn't believe the erotic yet caring quality to her exploration. He could feel his ball drawing up against his body as he approached his pinnacle of pleasure and gritted his teeth trying to stem the tide. He didn't want it to end so soon.

Finally, he could take no more. "Condom?"

She gave him a slight frown. "I don't think we need it, do we? I've only been with Trev for close to a year and we always used one. And I've had a clean bill of health in the meantime."

"Me too, and you know you're the only one I've been with in over a year, so…"

"I vote no."

God, the thought of being in her bare was combustible. Colin sat on the bed, pulled her towards him and kissed her lingeringly, shifting her with his hands around her waist until she straddled his lap.

Colin stroked her and found her already slick with need. He smiled against her mouth. "You're one sexy woman."

"Mmm…"

He slowly entered her while deepening their kiss. He paused a few times to allow her adjust to his cock, letting her channel flow and flex around him until he was seated to the hilt. Then he held still, firmly pressed into her, and kissed her thoroughly as he cupped her breasts and tweaked her pale, responsive nipples into hard peaks that brushed against his chest. Finally able to worship her beautiful body, he wanted to bring her as high as he was.

She moaned and moved on his cock and that was the end of his control. He finally obliged, grasping her hips and beginning a rocking motion that had his cock moving more within her than actually withdrawing and entering. He made slight circles as he thrust, and thrummed his fingers over her clit in time with his motions. Soon she was gasping with every pass.

Erica clutched him close as her head fell back, then she was coming, her head snapping forward and teeth grazing his shoulder as she ground her pelvis against his. Her channel pulsed, milking his cock and he couldn't hold back any longer. A handful of hard thrusts and his cum jetted into her as he groaned his completion, each pulsing movement made more intense by the stillness of the rest of their bodies.

Colin tried to catch his breath, swamped by the love he felt for Erica. Resting his cheek against her hair as they recovered, he felt a sense of rightness being there with her. Thank God Trevor had straightened things out and had got everything out in the open.

He picked her up and, still connected, began walking towards the bathroom. They had almost made it before he slipped out.

"Damn."

Erica giggled. "We'll just have to do it again sometime."

He let her down slowly and she stood naked and confident before him. "I love you," he whispered in the still of the room.

"I love you too." Erica stroked her hand across his cheek. "Thank you for not giving up on me when I was being stupid and short-sighted."

"How could I? You're the perfect woman for me. My forever woman." Tears filled Erica's eyes and alarm spiked through him. "What's wrong?"

She shook her head, eyes glistening. "Happy tears," she explained, fanning her face with one hand.

He caught her hand and kissed each of her eyelids in turn. "So that's what happiness tastes like. Salty."

They laughed and Colin reflected as he started the shower that happiness did seem to be a tangible thing now, because the sound of their mingled laughter had an almost palpable, wonderful feel to it.

Chapter Twelve

They hadn't poked their heads out of Erica's room until late that night. Trevor's bedroom door had been closed when they'd tiptoed out to the kitchen to warm up leftover Chinese, which was about the best thing Erica had ever tasted. Maybe she was just biased, since she was the happiest she'd ever been.

The next day her alarm had seemed to go off extremely early, and she'd heartily wished that she didn't have to go to work. Having Colin in bed with her was a temptation to snuggle and play hooky if she'd ever known one. He'd helped her out by getting up with her and encouraging her on her way out of the door.

The only consolation she'd had was that she had a lighter schedule at the moment story-wise, unless something major happened — fingers and toes crossed against that. And it had worked. She'd been able to leave work at an entirely reasonable time in the early evening.

Now the three of them were sitting around the living room after a nice dinner that Colin had made. She and

Colin were nestled together on the couch, and Trevor was lounging in an arm chair while they planned his move back to the condo.

"If I didn't know better, I'd feel very unwanted and unloved right now." Trevor pouted.

Erica smirked. "Oh, you know you'll be happy to get back to the man cave."

"No, really. I'd rather stay here. You never know when a live sex show is going to break out and the food is awesome."

"Speaking of sex..." Erica stopped talking when both of the guys burst into laughter. "What?"

"Nice segue," Colin teased.

"Best ever," Trevor agreed. "Keep talking. I want to see where this is going."

Erica fought a smile. The recent events seemed to have settled things between them and all of them, herself included, were crazy happy and content. It was a vast improvement on the past month or so when the future had been impenetrable.

"We need to talk about the having kids thing." God, here she was about two minutes into a relationship and already angling for kids. "I'm... Well, I'm not getting any younger."

"I know," Colin agreed, and laughed as she smacked his arm. "I don't mind starting trying right away."

Relief suffused her and she looked at Trevor, who was watching from his chair with a naughty grin. "I think your brother is willing to do the honors, although I'm not sure what changed his mind. He seemed very adamant about not being a donor anymore."

Trevor's grin softened into a smile, but his eyes dropped. "I made that decision after the accident." He looked up at Colin then back at Erica. "With him wanting to have kids but not able to produce sperm anymore, I knew my only donations from that time on would be to his future wife. Although" — the wicked glint returned — "I didn't count on being so lucky as to have the option to donate in person. Or as Rhonnie called it, hand-deliver." Trevor winked and Erica felt her cheeks go warm. "Much more enjoyable prospect than the old magazine and cup routine."

"Yeah, well, we'll just keep your enjoyment to the necessary minimum," Colin grumbled, though his contented tone belied the implied jealousy.

"Another thing. We've always used condoms, and — "

Trevor was already nodding. "No worries. I got tested last week — had a feeling this might come up. Or maybe I should say I hoped it would. No diseases so we're good to go."

Erica blinked at his preparedness. Really, between assuredness of the two brothers, she felt like she was constantly catching up. "Okay, well that's good."

Something else suddenly occurred to her. "Along those lines, I know at some point you're probably going to date someone else, but if we're going bare…"

How did you ask a young single guy to remain monogamous to you when you weren't even dating him?

"I get it, and I'm willing to put off sex with another partner until I've done what I've *come* here to do." He waggled his eyebrows at the pun and Colin and Erica groaned. "Best case scenario for all of us is to knock you up ASAP."

Feeling like the luckiest woman in the world, Erica thought about her future now with a sense of wonderment and expectation. In love with one brother, and loving them both, together they'd grow a family.

She eyed the hallway to the bedroom then sent what she hoped to be an inviting look to both of her men. "No time like the present."

Colin rose from the couch and met Trevor's inquiring look with a shrug. He honestly wasn't sure how he'd react when the time came, but he was going to try his damnedest to keep any jealousy at bay so he could give her this.

He pulled Erica to her feet and led the way, repeatedly kissing her on the way to the bedroom, putting all the love he had for her in every touch of his lips. As his arousal grew, the light kisses were no longer enough. He cupped the back of her head, pulling her in for a deep kiss, thrusting his tongue in to duel with her, needing the passionate response she was always willing to give him.

In the bedroom, Erica reached down and helped Colin unfasten then slide his jeans to his ankles, smoothing her hand down his backside and thighs with a touch that left him breathless. She tugged him down on the bed then knelt down in front of him to remove his boots and slip the pants off. Colin impatiently tore his T-shirt over his head and sat naked, his growing erection jutting out. A soft warmth enclosed his cock and he groaned as Erica slid her mouth down over the head then pulled off.

"Sit up against the headboard," she instructed then turned to Trevor while she quickly stripped. He watched her with a slight smile and Colin knew he should probably feel jealous, but thankfully he was so far avoiding that emotion.

"And where do you want me, boss lady?"

"Hmm, well, you undressing would be a good start and then we'll see," she answered then crawled up the bed towards Colin, pressing his legs apart until they were spread wide. A sensuous grin crossed her lips as she looked up at Colin from under her dark lashes and cupped Colin's sac in her small hands. She stroked his scar and rolled his ball in a manner that was fast becoming a regular part of their bed play, and went a long way towards assuaging the last of Colin's negative feelings about his body.

"Is this all right?" she teased, and he groaned.

"Erica, baby, if it were any more right, I'd be tossing you down and fucking you, and to hell with Trevor trying to get you pregnant."

She ran her fingers along the sensitive crease above his thighs then loosely held his cock. Erica looked fascinated as clear liquid welled from his slit, and she slid her hand up to touch it, rubbing it over the head of his cock in a super light, teasing touch that was driving him insane. When she lifted her finger to her mouth for a taste, Trevor and Colin groaned in unison.

Trevor was now as naked as they were and he joined them on the bed. "Sorry, Colin, I had no idea she was that much of a tease. I think turnabout is fair play, don't you?"

Colin was moving before the last few words were out of Trevor's mouth. He arranged Erica into an almost identical position as he'd been in against the headboard, only lying flat, then ran his whisker-rough cheek over the inside of her thigh. She gasped in response, and he inhaled her sweet scent as he laved the scratched area with his tongue, licking in tight circles closer and closer to the trimmed, red curls of her pussy.

He sucked at her smooth outer folds then used his thumbs to spread her labia apart, stroking the sleekness he uncovered with his tongue and his thumbs in turn. She squirmed restively and he stilled her with an iron grip on her hips then ran his tongue up to her clit, teasing it until it was swollen and taut.

Meanwhile, Trevor had moved to Erica's side and was tonguing and nipping across one pale breast. He watched as Trevor stroked the other with his hand, plucking the nipple to a tight stand. Colin turned his attention to Erica, who was watching both men with desire-hazed eyes.

Colin lapped lower at the new burst of moisture that was his for the taking then took the entire area around her swollen bud in his mouth and suckled and tongued it mercilessly until she was crying out and heaving helplessly against him as she came.

He barely allowed her to come down before slowly entering her with both thumbs, stretching her sensitive entrance and again flicking her nub with his tongue, keeping her off balance before withdrawing his touch completely and watching in satisfaction as her pussy attempted to grasp his retreating fingers.

"Nice," Trevor praised. Trevor dipped in to lick her clit once, and Colin heard Erica catch her breath. Then both men moved their attention upwards, suckling and lapping at her breasts, paying extra attention to her sensitive nipples.

Trevor moved between her thighs and cupped Erica's curvy ass with one hand as he used the other to place his shaft at the entrance of her pussy.

Colin rested his cheek against hers as he draped himself atop her while Trevor pressed deep inside her with a slow, steady motion. She linked her arms around his neck.

"Okay?" he asked, pulling back to look down at her, and she nodded. He braced himself on his elbows above her and gave her a tender kiss. He reached down between Trevor and Erica to get a thumb on her clit, riding it there, letting it stroke on each thrust.

Her eyes locked on his as she moaned and came with head thrown back and back arched. Her climax seemed to trip Trevor's orgasm, and he and Erica strained together, gasping their fulfilment.

Soon afterward, they shifted positions until Trevor was spooned behind Erica with Colin in front, kissing her full mouth periodically as they relaxed, sated. Colin was relieved that the experiment with sharing Erica's attentions had gone well and without any unexpected negative reactions. He supposed that the love between them all, though it varied in intensity and type on each side of the triangle, kept things from becoming too difficult.

This just might work out after all.

Epilogue

"Is Trevor home from LA yet? I haven't heard from him at all today." Erica dodged other pedestrians as she walked along the sidewalk towards Rhonnie's restaurant.

"No, I don't think he'll be back until tonight sometime. And it's a good thing I'm not a jealous man with how concerned you are about my brother's whereabouts." Colin's voice held a teasing grin.

"Not concerned, just curious, and you know I talk to you way more than I ever did to him." So much so that she'd had to set herself a strong rule to not reach out to Colin while she was at work or she'd never get anything done. It was tempting since he worked from the home office he'd set up in her former guest room, and he had never yet turned a call away because he was too busy to talk. That didn't stop her from having him on speed dial the moment she stepped out of the building for lunch or at the end of the day.

"So you're meeting Rhon for lunch?" he asked.

"Yes. Wish you could join us."

"Hmm. I'd love to see you too, but I'm heading out in about an hour to give a proposal presentation to that new client, and I need to wrap things up."

"Okay, okay, I'll let you go." She had just reached the restaurant anyway. "Love you."

"Love you too, babe."

"Knock 'em dead." She grinned at his laugh in reply and they said their goodbyes. She tucked her phone back into the slot of her purse and reached for the door. It flew open and she stepped back.

"Thank God you're finally here!" A waitress she knew by sight but not by name grabbed Erica by the hand and tugged her inside.

"What? Is Rhonnie okay?" Immediately concerned, she rushed after the girl, who headed straight back through the doors to the kitchen.

As soon as they entered the surprisingly quiet kitchen—it was the lunch rush and she could almost hear a pin drop—she heard Rhonnie's stressed-out voice, shouting, "How the hell you thought this was a good idea is beyond me!"

Erica burst into Rhonnie's office and stopped dead. Rhonnie was bent nearly in half, breathing heavily, with one palm flat on her desk and clutching the phone with her other hand. *Oh man*. Her usually unflappable friend was evidently in labour and falling apart at the seams. She could hear a masculine voice on the other end of the line and she plucked the phone from Rhon's unresisting grasp, running her other hand soothingly along her friend's shoulder.

"Barry?" she asked, cutting his placating voice off.

"Er? Oh thank fuck. She's having a meltdown and won't listen to anyone. Get her to go to the hospital already, would you? I'll meet you there."

"Tell him to bring the car seat! They won't let me bring her home without the car seat!" Erica winced as Rhon yelled right in her ear.

"God! Yes! I will bring everything. Tell her, Erica. And get her out of the office!"

After assuring Barry she'd get her there, Erica hung up and looked around. Rhon had her hand in a death grip and groaned. Erica knew that first babies always took a long time to come but who knew how long Rhonnie had been at this?

"Rhon. I need my hand back, hon. Let's go have a baby, okay?"

Rhonnie met her gaze. She looked terrified. "I changed my mind. I can't do this."

"Oh, come here." She pulled Rhonnie into a hug. "You can and you will. Don't you want to meet this little sweetheart you've been taking such good care of for this long? I know I do."

Rhon gulped in a breath then another and finally nodded.

"Good." How the hell was she going to get Rhon to her car? *The hell with it*, she decided, and she pulled out her phone to call her assistant. Within minutes she'd cleared her schedule for the day and arranged for a hired car to pick them up in the service alley.

She sat with Rhon while they waited for the text. Her friend seemed to have got herself a bit more under control and she gave rational orders left and right to her relieved staff. Erica smiled as she wondered how together she would feel when her time came.

"And what are you laughing at?" Rhon scowled at her, but there was little heat in her tone.

"Oh, just trying to decide whether I'll freak out in about seven and a half months." She braced herself.

"What? And you're just now telling me? Jesus." Rhon smacked her hard then abruptly pulled her into a hug. She backed away enough to look down between them at Erica's still flat stomach with a smile. "Seven and half months. You guys didn't waste any time, did you?"

Erica shook her head, tearing up a bit at the joy in her friend's expression. "No—probably happened the first time without the condom."

"La, la, la." Rhon covered her ears. "I don't want to hear about the yucky mechanics of it. Ugh."

Erica's phone pinged, and she glanced at it to confirm it was the car service. "The limo's out back. Can you walk okay?"

"Yeah, I think so. Ooh, first class service. Oh"—Rhonnie stopped short halfway to standing—"grab the towel out of my hospital bag. I don't want my water to break all over the nice seats. I mean, if it was just a taxi, I wouldn't care but…"

Erica laughed and lifted the bag. "Come on, mama. Let's get you there."

* * * *

Around midnight, they had just been moved from Rhonnie's birthing suite to her permanent room when a knock came on the door. "You have a visitor." One of the nurses came in, followed closely by Colin.

"Hi, sweetheart." He set a colourful arrangement of flowers on the side table and gave Rhon a kiss on the forehead. Then he took Erica into his arms and she went limp against his welcome strength. "Tired?"

"Very. But wound up, too, all at the same time."

He walked her over to the padded bench along the wall, sat and pulled her down onto his lap. She rested her head on his broad shoulder. As was becoming a habit, he ran his hand down to her abdomen. She smiled against his neck.

"Have you told Rhon yet?" he whispered into her ear and she nodded in response.

"Gave her plenty to yell at me about. It was probably a good distraction."

"I wasn't yelling," Rhonnie protested from the bed. After a briefly raising an eyebrow at Erica, her eyes went straight back to the small bundle in Barry's arms where he was sitting in the glider.

"Have you named her yet?" Colin asked and Erica laughed. Rhon and Barry had been arguing for months about names and hadn't resolved anything yet.

"Sounds like you're having fun in here." Trevor came striding into the room unannounced, carrying a giant stuffed elephant with balloons attached to its collar. The nurse turned around from where she was taking Rhon's vitals, startled, then looked back and forth between the brothers. Her eyebrows shot up when Trevor went straight to Erica and kissed her lingeringly on the mouth as she sat on his twin's lap, but she didn't say anything, just gave a quick shake of her head and turned her attention back to her task.

"Hi, sweets. You look exhausted. Can we take you home? You need to be resting. Oh…" He straightened and eyed Rhonnie while loudly asking Erica, "Have you told her yet?"

"Yes, damn it. She finally let me in on the secret that everyone else in the freaking world knew."

"I didn't know," Barry pointed out.

"I just wanted you to enjoy your time in the spotlight. I wasn't going to tell you until after you took…what's-her-face home." Erica waved her hand in a *see-what-I-mean* gesture. "Seriously, you need to choose a name, Rhon."

Rhonnie looked at Barry and cocked her head, but didn't say a word.

Barry sighed. "Fine. Have it your way." His expression was resigned but quickly softened as he looked back at their sleeping daughter.

Rhonnie smiled triumphantly. "Thank you. Elizabeth it is."

"Why was that so hard to decide on?" Trevor asked with a curious look. He stepped aside to give the nurse room to get by on her way out of the room.

"They're gonna call her Liz, I just know it," Barry warned. "I hate that name." He shuddered. "I have a friend with a sister named Liz and she's a total b—"

"Don't swear in front of the baby," Rhonnie interrupted. "They'll call her whatever we call her. There are a kazillion different nicknames for Elizabeth. Eliza, Beth…"

Erica tuned her friend's list out as Colin murmured in her ear, "Do you think we'll have as much trouble deciding on a name?" Colin's breath on her neck sent shivers down her spine.

"Hmm. I don't know. There'll be three of us trying to agree." Erica glanced up at Trevor to find him completely still and staring at them. "What?"

"You'll let me help pick a name?"

"Of course. You're going to be the dad just as much as Colin."

Trevor looked at Colin, who nodded. He slowly grinned. "Cool. I'll start coming up with ideas. Oh…I'll make a list."

"Oh brother." Colin shook his head, but tried to look innocent when Trevor mimed, "*What?*"

"You guys suck."

They all looked at Rhonnie, who was angrily dashing tears from her cheeks. She held her hand out, palm facing them. "No. Just go. You are way too emotionally sappy for me right now."

Erica rose and crossed to give Rhon a hug after pushing her arm to the side. "I think we'll let you guys bond and all that. Try to get some rest, okay, hon?"

"Fat chance in here with these sadistic nurses, but I appreciate the sentiment. You need some rest too. Take your boys home and straight to bed with you. And no funny business." She gave the brothers a half-serious glare. "Bad enough you already got her in the condition she's in. Do you know how much it hurts when—?"

"And I'll call you tomorrow and probably come by," Erica hastily interjected as Colin and Trevor paled. "Night, mama. Good night, Barry. And you too, baby Elizabeth." She walked over to give Barry and the baby a quick hug too, then waited for the guys to say their farewells. They all walked out together and silently made their way to the elevator.

Erica's thoughts were full of all that had happened and what was to come in her own life, so it was a few minutes before the continued quiet finally registered.

"Okay, guys. What's on your minds? Not that last bit about it hurting." She linked her hands with theirs and tugged them off the elevator once they'd reached the quiet main floor.

They looked at each other across the top of her head while they walked towards the lobby, then Colin slid his arm around her waist. "I hate the thought of you being in pain." Trevor somberly nodded his agreement.

Erica smiled at their worried expressions that made them look so alike. "Well, yeah, it'll probably hurt like hell." She was looking at Colin and he winced. She continued, "But it'll be brief and the reward to me is well worth it. I wouldn't wish away any part of it." A happy thought occurred to her. "You know, probably the next time we all go out these doors at the same time, there'll be four of us instead of three."

The thought made her catch her breath, and she gave each of the brothers a squeeze — Colin around his waist and Trevor by the hand she was holding. She was smiling as she began to cross the walkway towards the parking structure.

"Or maybe five…"

About the Author

After living all over the US while growing up, I've settled into the beautiful Pacific Northwest and can't see myself living anywhere else. I'm a mom to two girls, who—to my pride and gratification—love to read and want to make a living with words themselves someday.

Even when I'm not writing, I find myself storing up experiences and people for future reference. I had decades of potential material at my mental fingertips by the time I started putting my stories into words.

I believe that passion is to be treasured, stepping out of the box should be encouraged, and forever can come from the most unlikely of beginnings. So find a story, step inside and immerse yourself in the magic of love. I'll meet you there…

Stacey Lynn Rhodes loves to hear from readers. You can find her contact information, website details and author profile page at http://www.totallybound.com.

Totally Bound Publishing